Nurse In The South Seas

by

Sheila Ridley

Dales Large Print Books
Long Preston, North Yorkshire,
BD23 4ND, England.

British Library Cataloguing in Publication Data.

Ridley, Sheila
    Nurse in the South Seas.

    A catalogue record of this book is
    available from the British Library

    ISBN   1-84262-474-1 pbk
    ISBN   978-1-84262-474-6 pbk

First published in Great Britain in 1965 by Robert Hale Ltd.

Copyright © Sheila Ridley 1965

The moral right of the author has been asserted

Published in Large Print 2006 by arrangement with
Robert Hale Limited

678359

Dales Large Print is an imprint of Library Magna Books Ltd.

Printed and bound in Great Britain by
T.J. (International) Ltd., Cornwall, PL28 8RW

NURSE IN THE SOUTH SEAS

NURSE IN THE SOUTH SEAS

Helen Davis, S.R.N., does not long for adventure, nor travel to faraway places. She is perfectly happy living in her native North Wales and when her friend Mair tells her she is only half-alive, Helen is unmoved. Yet, somehow, she finds herself taking a job in the exotic South Pacific, meeting people unlike any she has known – Colin Fraser, the light-hearted, irresponsible young island doctor, and medical officer Paul Strang, so sternly efficient. She comes up against problems and mystery, too. Helen did not seek travel, adventure or romance ... they just happened to her.

Chapter One

Helen Davis, S.R.N., came into the changing-room of Llandelly Cottage Hospital humming cheerfully. She undressed quickly and put on the blue and white uniform that became her slim figure and fair colouring well. As she was pinning on her cap, the door was flung open and another staff-nurse, plump and red-haired, bounced in.

'You sound happy,' she said accusingly to Helen.

'Aren't you? It's your half-day.'

'I know, and it's pouring down as usual!' The newcomer, Mair Phillips, walked across to the window, taking off her apron as she went. 'Honestly, there can't be another place in the whole world where it rains as much as it does here in North Wales! It just never stops!'

'Oh, Mair!' Helen laughed. 'Anyway, you can't have fresh green valleys without rain.'

'I don't mind some; it's this continual downpour I object to,' the other girl pointed out aggrievedly. She finished undressing and then, down to her slip, surveyed herself in a long mirror. 'D'you think I'm losing weight?'

'No,' came the candid reply, and she bridled.

'There's charming you are!' Then she studied her reflection again and said, 'Well, if I am fatter, it's the stodgy food they give us here. I don't know how you keep so thin. Or perhaps it's boredom that makes me eat too much.' She sighed deeply, and went to a wardrobe and took out a brown woollen dress. She pulled it over her head and thrust her arms with difficulty through the sleeves, talking all the time. 'Now I've got to walk nearly half a mile to the bus stop and travel for an hour to get to a town. Town! I mean, somewhere bigger than two cottages and a chapel! Well, it's not good enough! I don't know how I've stood it so long. When I think I've wasted four years of my young life on the desert air of this – this neck of the back-woods!' She was quiet for a minute, then looking solemnly at her friend, announced, 'I've made up my mind.'

Helen nodded abstractedly. 'Tell me about it later, love. It's nearly two o'clock.' She glanced into the mirror and smoothed the fringe of fair hair that curved across her forehead. 'I must go now.'

'Oh, don't go just yet. Listen–'

'Sorry, but it's Mr Irvine's afternoon and you know what a flap Sister Potts gets into when the great specialist is due. Is it important?'

With assumed nonchalance, Mair said, 'Just that I'm leaving.'

'And where are you off to this time Tangier? Madeira? Or–'

'The South Sea Islands.'

'Well, that's a change,' Helen commented lightly. Mair had these 'away-from-it-all' fits roughly once a month and they usually lasted about two or three days, evaporating either with an improvement in the weather or when she met a new and interesting young man. Yet – was there a difference on this occasion? Did she mean it? There was certainly a great deal of determination in the set of her chin and in the way she spoke. But no – it was ridiculous! The South Sea Islands of all places! It was just another whim. Mair would have forgotten the whole thing before the week was over.

As if she could guess Helen's thoughts, Mair asserted, 'I'm serious, you know.' She wandered back to the window and leaned against the frame, tracing the zig-zag course of a rain-drop down the window-pane. 'Imagine it,' she said dreamily, 'an island in the sun. Blue lagoons, swaying palms, golden sands–'

'Mosquitoes–' Helen put in, and was ignored.

'–hibiscus, frangipani–'

'–hurricanes–'

'–mangoes, paw-paw, breadfruit–'

'–malaria–'

'–haunting music and – oh, Helen, think of it! To be thousands of miles from this–' she gestured with an arm towards the dripping scene beyond the window as she turned her back on it, 'this dreariness! To be finished with these ghastly things!' she added, shaking a plastic mackintosh angrily from its folds.

'Ghastly or not, be careful or you'll split it,' Helen warned.

The other nurse gazed at her in silence for a moment. Then, 'I simply don't understand you,' she confessed, with a mixture of bewilderment and despair. 'You seem quite content to bury yourself here in Llandelly for the rest of your life. It's shameful, when you could do so much better for yourself. You're pretty, you've a figure I'd give anything for, and on top of that, you're intelligent.'

Helen made a little curtsey. 'Thanks very much, but I happen to be perfectly happy

10

where I am. I like North Wales. It's beautiful.'

'It's dull,' Mair countered.

'It has mountains, lakes–'

'Rain–'

'–soft, gentle voices–'

'–narrow minds, rain–'

'–stirring music and – oh, Mair!' They laughed and then Helen said she really had to get to the ward.

'And I must commence the long, long trail to the bus stop.'

They went out of the room together and before they parted at the head of a flight of stairs, Mair repeated, 'I'm really serious. I'm giving my notice in and then it's – South Sea Islands, here I come!' And she ran down the stairs and out into the rain.

As the door banged behind her, Helen smiled. Where on earth would the crazy girl take it into her head to go next?

It was three weeks later, a clear, sunny day of early March, when Mair came into the changing-room with a letter in her hand and an anxious expression on her round face. Helen was there changing out of uniform and, when the letter was handed to her, she sat down to read it, frowning slightly.

The heading was 'Commonwealth Medical Commission', and it thanked Nurse Phillips for her enquiry regarding nursing posts in the Pacific Islands and went on to say that there was a vacancy in one of the smaller Polynesian islands and, as it was a matter of some urgency that this be filled, it was hoped to arrange an interview and medical tests with the least possible delay.

Helen's blue eyes skimmed over the words twice before she returned the letter. 'Well, so you did mean it, after all,' she said slowly. 'You didn't tell me you'd done anything about it. I thought you'd dropped the idea.'

'I wrote that same day – you remember I was pretty fed up with everything.' Mair folded the letter carefully and put it back into the envelope. 'I already had the address.'

'You've got what you wanted then. You must be excited.' Helen bent to take off her working shoes and stockings, adding, 'They want you to go almost at once. Have you started preparing yet?'

'Er – no, I haven't.'

'You'll need to get a move on, won't you? When did you give your notice in?'

Mair bit her lip. 'About three weeks ago – but I withdrew it.'

'You–?' Helen sat up and stared at her

friend. 'Why?'

'Because – I don't want to leave–' came the hesitant explanation, 'not now.'

'Oh.' Picking up a pair of nylons from a chair beside her, Helen began to examine them closely for snags. She was aware that the other girl was blushing vividly, but kept her eyes on the stockings while she asked, 'Something to do with a certain young farmer you've been meeting rather frequently over the past fortnight?'

Mair laughed shyly. 'Yes – among other things. I've known David for ages, but we never really noticed each other until the Institute dance. Now somehow everything's changed. You know how it is.' Helen gave her an understanding smile, as if she did indeed know 'how it is', and stifled the envy that sprang in her to see such utter happiness. 'I used to think Llandelly was the most dismal spot on earth,' Mair went on softly. 'I must have been mad. It's a beautiful place.'

'I quite agree. You'd better send a telegram to these people and let them know you're not interested in their tropical island any longer.'

'I can't do that,' Mair said, flopping into a chair and resting her chin on her hand. 'You read the letter. They need a nurse urgently.

I can't suddenly tell them I don't want to go, after saying how keen I was only a short time ago. I'd look pretty silly, and it would be letting them down badly.'

'What are you going to do then? Go to the other side of the world and leave David?'

The suggestion sent a spasm of pain across Mair's face. 'I can't do that either.' She looked at the floor for a minute and then up at Helen. 'There is a way of solving both problems – to avoid letting the Medical Commission down, without my parting from David.'

'If you take him out there with you, you mean?'

'Ha! It would be easier to transplant Harlech Castle! Good gracious, no! David's roots go ten miles deep into the soil of his beloved farm.'

'Well then?' Helen stood up to see if the seams of her stockings were straight and was adjusting one when the reply came.

'I thought if you went instead of me–'

'Me?' she repeated in astonishment. 'I don't want to go. I'm sorry. I'd like to help, but I wouldn't dream of going all that way from home.'

'Why not? There's nothing to keep you here. Your parents are still quite young;

you've no special boy-friend. Honestly, Helen bach, I do think you ought to go; not to get me out of a fix, but for your own sake.' Mair's eyebrows drew together as she looked critically at the other nurse. 'You've been in a rut too long,' she finished bluntly.

The allegation was denied emphatically but in vain. 'What else can you call it? You've lived your whole life within a few miles of this hospital among people you've known since you were born practically. Even on holidays you've never done anything more adventurous than spending a week with your auntie in Anglesey. Don't you want to see other places, meet different people? Don't you ever wonder about the world outside your own parish?'

'I like my parish.'

'Fair enough. But that's no reason to em-balm yourself in it. How can you love Wales who only Wales know? I'd jump at the oppor-tunity if I were in your shoes.'

Helen sighed. 'You're different from me. I just wouldn't know what to do with myself so far from everything I'm used to. Besides, there's the choir, and my Red Cross work, and–'

Mair Phillips threw up her hands in despair. 'Helen, Helen, really! There's been a choir at St Michael's for centuries; it's not going to collapse because one mediocre soprano leaves. And I'm sure someone else can be found to give weekly chats to your Red Cross cadets on applying a tourniquet and bathing a baby. No, love,' she shook her head sadly, 'the trouble with you is that you're afraid to get out of your comfortable, familiar groove. You're only half-alive, and it's shocking for an attractive, healthy girl of twenty-three to put safety first when there are so many exciting things to do and see!'

Chapter Two

These words of Mair's were in Helen's mind
as she stood at the rail of a crowded launch
that skimmed across the turquoise waters of
a reef and came to a jolting halt on gleaming
white sand. Beyond, purple-grey mountains
were clothed in forests of rich, deep green.

This was it, she thought, gripping the rail
tightly to keep her balance and also for the
confidence it gave her. It was something to
hold on to, in this strange new world of brilliant sunshine and noise.

So many exciting things. It was true, of
course. This was exciting, arriving here on
Queen Victoria Island, a colourful mass of
rock and coral thrusting up through the
calm of the blue Pacific; the bustling, gaily-
dressed people pushing past her to jump
down to the palm-dotted beach and be
greeted by other laughing, brown-skinned
islanders. The journey had been exciting,
too. The long train trip from Llandelly to
London to board the jet that brought her to
New Zealand, then the third stage by steam-

ship to Prince Albert, the largest in this string of coral isles and atolls known as the Royalty Islands. And here she was at her journey's end. They say journeys end in lovers meeting, she thought vaguely. Oh, it was all wonderfully exciting – or would be if only she didn't feel so horribly nervous!

'Oh!' she exclaimed, as a hand touched her bare arm, and she turned to find herself looking into the friendly, welcoming face of a woman – a small, middle-aged, grey-haired woman, wearing an old-fashioned navy cotton dress and flat brown sandals. This must be Mrs McFarlane, Helen decided. She knew the Rev. Angus McFarlane was in charge of the island mission.

'You'll be Nurse Davis,' the woman said, and subjected the Welsh girl to a brief, but thorough scrutiny. Slim, she was – possibly too delicate for the job she had taken on, or was it her fairness that made her appear fragile? Neatly dressed, in her simple white frock and sensible shady hat. Pretty, with a perfect complexion and lovely blue eyes – very pretty. Hm – that could be unfortunate, but the Medical Commission could hardly turn down a qualified applicant on those grounds, particularly when the post urgently needed filling and there was no other suitable applicant. Time would tell. She certainly looked a nice girl, and was obviously frightened. 'I'm Margaret McFarlane,' the woman said, taking Helen's hand in a firm clasp, 'Bit of a mouthful, isn't it? Call me Meg.'

Helen smiled. She was feeling a little less nervous. With this kindly woman to help her she might cope reasonably well. 'I had a letter saying that I'd be able to stay with you,' she said. 'It's very nice of you and your husband to offer–'

Her thanks were brushed aside cheerfully. 'Not at all, ma dear. We'll enjoy having you. But I mustn't keep you here blethering after the long journey you've had. Wales, you come from, is it no'? We're from Scotland oursel's – if you hadna guessed!' she chuckled. 'Now–' she looked towards the beach where a score or so of grinning children were standing in two lines facing each other, boys on one side, girls opposite. The girls waited fairly patiently in their starched white dresses, only scuffling their feet and giggling shyly; but the boys shoved and jostled each other as the waiting became tedious. One or two of the bolder spirits waved thin brown arms towards the launch and Mrs McFarlane smiled and waved back.

'Those are my star pupils – I run a wee school here,' she explained to Helen. 'The whole lot wanted to be on the welcoming committee to greet you, but I put my foot down and said only the extra good ones could come. Mercy me! I didn't know imps could turn into angels so quickly!' She put her arm through Helen's. 'Come along now. You must be tired, but we'll soon be home.'

The instant the two women stepped on to the sand, the children rushed to them, laughing and chattering and wreathing Helen's neck with a brilliance of frangipani, jasmine and hibiscus blossoms. In their exuberance they knocked her hat askew and she took it off, shaking her hair. They stared, and she glanced questioningly at Mrs Mc-Farlane.

'It's your hair,' the Scotswoman told her. 'Most of them have never seen a blonde girl before. They'll probably have lots of questions to ask when they know you a little better; they're insatiably curious.' To the tallest of the boys she said, 'Riki, get the others to help you load Nurse Davis's luggage into the trap.'

Eagerly the youngsters fell upon the baggage and transferred it to a shabby, blue-painted cart that stood, a piebald pony between its shafts, a few yards away.

Mrs McFarlane went to tickle the pony's nose. 'We can't afford a car, but we'd rather have Robbie anyway. He'll have us home in a brace of shakes.'

Shakes was apt, Helen reflected, as the none-too-sturdy wagon crammed with as many of the children as could possibly squeeze aboard rattled its merry way along the white coral road. Flame trees bent their branches above to form a cool archway, so that when they emerged into the full glare of the afternoon sun, Helen had to reach hastily for her hat.

A few minutes later they were all tumbling out of the trap in front of a square, single-storied house standing in a large unkempt garden on the side of a gently-sloping hill. The house was built mainly of weatherboard and had once been painted white; the roof was red and looked too heavy for the walls to support, and the unserviceable-looking shutters were green. Bougainvillea in every imaginable shade of pink, blue and yellow entwined lavishly the rails of the wide verandah and flowed over on to the eaves.

Her hostess got down and held out a hand to Helen. 'It's no palace, but it's certainly colourful,' she said happily. To the children she said there would be biscuits in the kitchen for them when they had put the luggage into the hall, and not to be late for school tomorrow.

As they ran around, tripping each other up, laughing, squabbling, but gradually getting the job done, a man came down the verandah steps. He was large, with a grizzled beard, and wore khaki shorts and shirt.

'Ah, here's Angus. I thought he'd be home by this,' said Mrs McFarlane.

The clergyman hurried towards Helen, smiling broadly. 'Welcome, welcome, ma dear,' he said, taking her hands in his. 'I'm sorry I couldna' be there to greet you off the boat, but I'm pairfectly sure you had a warm reception, forby.'

'I certainly did,' she assured him happily, easing the fragrant lei a little back from her neck.

'Ah?' Angus McFarlane cocked his huge head on one side and gazed consideringly at her. 'Do I detect the wee trace of a Welsh accent in that charming voice?' he demanded. 'Oh, well, it's no' your fault.'

His wife looked up at him. 'Away with your nonsense, Angus,' she reproved, 'the poor girl doesna know how to take you.' She patted Helen's arm, saying, 'He's only teasing. Now we'll go and see about some tea.'

They walked up to the house. Mrs Mc-Farlane asked Helen if she'd like a wash before tea and when the nurse said she would, led her into a cool, bare hall. Helen picked up a small suit-case from the collection of baggage the children had deposited there and followed the other woman through a slatted door into a passage and then into a bathroom. 'Your room is the next on the right as you go out of here, dear. Will you manage now? I'll leave you then and we'll have tea on the verandah as soon as you're ready.'

Left alone, Helen went to the window and pulled aside the net curtaining. She could see the mountains clearly from here as they rose from valleys of purple, stabbing the sky. How grand and proud they stood. And how different from the mountains of Wales.

Oh, dear, she caught herself up, she must not start getting homesick already!

After a quick bath, she put on a dress of pale yellow silk that was almost the same colour as her hair, and pinned a sprig of creamy frangipani from her lei to the shoulder. Coming out on to the verandah, she found her host and hostess relaxing in deck chairs in a shaded corner. A white-painted wicker table set for tea was between them and a third chair was drawn up.

Mr McFarlane got to his feet. 'Here you are, then. Looking as fresh as a daisy, too – or should I say a daffodil, in view of your nationality?'

Helen smiled and sat down. She had been lucky to find herself living with this delightful couple.

Over their second cups, Mrs McFarlane asked her for her first impressions of the island.

Helen looked around, from the riotously gay garden to the glistening blue of the ocean in the distance, with lush green bush between. 'It's beautiful,' she breathed. 'And the people are so happy and friendly. It's perfect.'

'Eh, not – quite – perfect,' Angus McFarlane said slowly, tugging at his beard. 'But we are very fortunate here on Victoria. Not all the Pacific Islands are as lucky. We have an excellent climate for most of the year, and the people still have some of the lovable simplicity that used to be characteristic of the islanders. Being small and off the beaten track, we have escaped the attentions of commercial interests that have brought

24

such changes – good and bad – to some islands. Of course, we have our share of health troubles.'

'Yes.' Helen sat forward and put her cup down. 'I don't really know very much about the work I'll be doing here. I came in such a rush that there was no time to find out all the things I ought to know, so I'll have to pick them up as I go along. I would have liked to meet the nurse who was here before me–' she glanced at her hostess, '–I suppose you knew her quite well?'

There was a slight frown on Meg Mc-Farlane's face as she said, 'Oh, yes. We saw a good deal of Georgina – Nurse Grey.'

'She must have hated leaving this lovely place. Had she been here long?'

'About a year.'

Something in the older woman's manner puzzled Helen. Was it embarrassment? Uneasiness of some sort was there. A definite reluctance to talk about the other nurse. What could the reason be? It would not do to probe, but she could not help wondering. Angus McFarlane had said Victoria Island was not perfect. Was she seeing evidence of another flaw in what had seemed a paradise on earth?

The noisy arrival of a battered red sports car at the gate put an end to her speculations. A tall young man jumped out and came jauntily up the garden path, hands in the pockets of his fawn drill jacket and shaking back his hair. Light brown hair that could do with the attention of a barber, Helen noted as he came nearer, but slight disapproval did not prevent her noticing too that he was rather handsome and had an attractive manner.

Mrs McFarlane said: 'Hello, Doctor. You're just in time to welcome our new nurse, Miss Davis.' She turned to the Welsh girl. 'Helen, this is Dr Fraser.'

'Colin Fraser,' the young man drawled, looking Helen up and down as be took her hand and obviously liking what he saw. 'The island grape-vine did not deceive me.'

'So it wasn't coincidence that brought you here,' Angus McFarlane remarked.

'Of course not. I don't believe in leaving things to chance,' the doctor smiled, his eyes still on Helen. She withdrew her hand from his and looked away, hoping her cheeks did not betray her embarrassment at his blatant show of admiration. He went on, 'I was up at the hospital when I heard that my new assistant had landed, and that she was more

26

than passing fair. Well, naturally, I lost no time in making her acquaintance.'

Helen smiled shyly. 'I'm sorry if I'm interrupting your work, Doctor.'

'Will you listen to the child! Apologising for being the most delightful excuse for downing tools I've had in months!'

'Since when have you needed an excuse?' Mrs McFarlane asked caustically. 'Anyway, are you going to have some tea now you are here? The pot's empty but I could make some fresh—'

'Ha!' Colin Fraser threw back his head and laughed wholeheartedly. 'So this is the famous Scottish hospitality we hear so much about! No, dear lady, thank you very much for your kind and pressing invitation,' he bowed deeply in her direction, 'but I have other plans for this glorious April afternoon.' He bowed again this time to Helen. 'I intend to take my charming colleague for a drive round the island,' he announced.

When the nurse cast a doubtful glance towards the somewhat dilapidated vehicle at the gate, he held up a warning hand. 'Don't! Don't say it!' he begged.

Her eye-brows went up. 'Say what?'

'What you were going to say. Harsh words trembled upon your tongue as you regarded

Jessie,' he said solemnly, waving a hand at the car. 'Bite them back, I implore you, for though she has been around – yes, I'll grant that she is not in her first youth and, as they say in the advertisements, it shows – still she has her feelings and I'm sure you will respect them, being a nicely brought up young lady.'

Mrs McFarlane stood up, her lips pursed. 'Helen has her feelings too, Doctor, and I imagine that just now she's feeling very tired and more inclined to rest than go off on a sight-seeing tour.' She turned to the girl for confirmation, but Helen hesitated.

'I – don't know. I–' Both alternatives had their appeal, and as she tried to think a tactful way out of the situation the matter was taken out of her hands.

'That settles it, then,' Colin Fraser said firmly. 'You'll enjoy the drive. Get your hat, darling.'

Rather than prolong the clash of wills, Helen went into the hall where her white hat and gloves were still on a bamboo table. Standing in front of the mirror to put them on, she could hear the voices of the three on the verandah; not the words, but the sound was unmistakably that of angry people.

When she rejoined them there was a brief strained silence.

The drive began in silence, too, and when the bungalow was well behind Helen glanced sideways at the doctor. His mouth was set in a thin line, and he stared unblinkingly ahead as they sped along a ribbon of white road between the sea and the forest. Eventually, though, his jaw relaxed and he leaned back in his seat.

Helen relaxed too, revelling in the freshness of the breeze and the warmth of the late afternoon sun on her face.

Reducing speed, Colin Fraser turned to look at her, smiling. 'Oh, it's impossible to be annoyed for long in a place like this.'

'Annoyed?' she asked innocently.

He laughed. 'Don't pretend you didn't notice that I was more than slightly steamed up when we set off, because I won't believe you're so insensitive.'

'Well, I know Mrs McFarlane was not really keen on my coming out with you. She would rather I'd rested.' Helen put this forward as convincingly as she could, but her explanation was greeted by a loud snort.

'Huh! You're darned right she didn't want you to come out with me, but it wasn't anything to do with your being tired. Meg McFarlane–' he said the name with a depth of bitterness that came as a nasty shock to the nurse, 'detests me! Nothing would please her more than to get me off the island for good!'

He pressed his foot viciously down on the accelerator and the car spurted forward, swerving dangerously near the edge of the road where the ground fell steeply away to the beach. 'Sorry,' he muttered, and pulled over to the other side of the road, slowing down and finally stopping in the shade of a spreading jacaranda tree.

Helen breathed in the sweet scent of its masses of blue-mauve flowers. She was trying to think of something to say to ease the tension, for the man beside her was gripping the steering wheel tightly and staring fixedly ahead. 'Have you a cigarette?' she asked, though she rarely smoked.

He gave her one and took one himself. Neither spoke for a while, then Colin Fraser said, 'I may as well tell you something about the situation here. You'll find out anyway, but I'd rather get my oar in first.'

'You make it sound as though there was a feud or something going on,' Helen said, with an attempt at lightness. 'I can't believe it's anything serious.'

'You can't, eh?' He tapped ash from his

cigarette carefully into the dashboard ashtray. 'That just shows what a lot you have to learn.'

'You said yourself it was impossible to be angry for long here,' she retorted. 'In any case, I'd rather you didn't tell me. If I'm to work here – and particularly while I'm living with the McFarlanes – I ought to keep out of any little disagreements there may be.'

He grinned at her, his charming self again. 'Very nicely said, my dear, and your sentiments do you credit, I'm sure. But don't tell me you aren't curious about the island scandal.'

Her head jerked round and she stared at him. 'Scandal?' she repeated sharply.

Chapter Three

Dr Fraser shrugged his wide shoulders. 'Perhaps I'm pitching it a bit strong. Call it gossip, if you like. In a community such as exists on Victoria that is certainly a force to reckon with.' The bitterness was back in his voice and Helen became more and more troubled as he went on, 'You'll find out about that soon enough, too, but I might as well put you on your guard. Not that I think you are likely to fall foul of the island code.' He paused and studied her closely for what seemed a long time, then said softly, 'One can never tell, of course. That's what makes people such fascinating creatures.'

'I – suppose so,' she murmured uncomfortably.

'Take yourself, for instance–'

'Me? Oh, goodness, I'm perfectly ordinary.'

'Well, apart from the fact that you're much prettier than most girls, I'd have probably agreed with you – don't be annoyed, darling – if I'd met you in – where is it? Llyndally? Llandilly? But you've come all this way alone to work among alien people at the tender age of – twenty-one? Well, twenty-three then. So you are by no means ordinary.'

'But that just happened,' she told him.

'How did it happen? I'd like to know.' He twisted round in his seat so that he was facing her and leaned one elbow on the back of the seat. 'I'd like to know all about you, in fact. And don't say there's nothing to tell, or I'll – I'll shoot you.' He took a banana from a bunch on the dashboard and pointed it menacingly at her. 'Talk!' he commanded.

She laughed and put up her hands. 'There isn't much to tell, honestly. You'll be awfully bored. Oh, all right – where shall I begin?'

'Begin,' he said portentously, 'at the beginning. You were born–?'

'Oh, yes,' she giggled, 'I was born. At my parents' farm near Llandelly. I have a brother, Arwel, and a cat, Ianto. I went to the village school and then to the High School at Harbourne. When I left, I began my training at the Cottage Hospital in Llandelly. Then I came here. That's all. The story of my life.'

'What about boy-friends? You're not going to ask me to believe that even in your quiet Welsh village the young men didn't notice a girl like you?'

'I had boy-friends, but no-one special. No-one new ever came to Llandelly. Everyone knew everyone else and their entire family–'

'So you decided to spread your wings?'

'Oh, no. It wasn't like that at all. I didn't come here because I was discontented. I love North Wales. I was quite happy to stay there. It was my friend, Mair Phillips, who wanted to come to the South Seas.'

'Where is she, then?'

'Still in Llandelly.'

'And you're here.' Colin scratched his head. 'I thought it was the Irish who were supposed to be illogical.'

She smiled. 'It's simple enough. Mair applied for this job, but by the time she got the reply she'd changed her mind. She'd fallen in love, you see, and didn't want to leave her boy-friend. The letter said the post urgently needed filling, so as I had no ties, I came.'

'And you think that, but for this chance happening, you'd have stayed put for ever more?'

'Yes. I liked my work, and the people. I was content.'

'Content! Contentment is for the old, Helen. No, I think you – subconsciously, perhaps – grasped this opportunity to break free. Anyway, I'm glad you did come.' He put a hand over hers. 'We needed you badly.'

She looked away. 'Thank you, Doctor. I hope I'll be able to help. Er – what are those?' she asked, pointing to a group of trees bearing clusters of what looked like orange blossom.

'Paw-paw,' he told her. 'The fruit's something like melon.'

'Oh. Does the blossom have a scent? I'd like to stretch my legs for a few minutes.' She opened the door and stepped on to the road. It felt hot beneath her thin sandals. The fragrance of the trees reached out to her, heady and intoxicating, as she walked to them. Then she stood still, her face raised, her eyes closed. Momentarily she had forgotten her companion and when he spoke she got a slight shock.

'Sorry, darling,' he said with a chuckle. 'I didn't mean to make you jump. I won't offer you a penny for your thoughts. I'm sure they're worth much more. You were miles away.'

'No, I wasn't dreaming. At least–' she hesitated, trying to recall exactly what had been in her mind when he approached her, but unable to. 'I don't know.'

She was surprised when he nodded understandingly and murmured, 'So it's got you already, has it?' He looked searchingly into her deep blue eyes and nodded again. 'Yes, my diagnosis is confirmed. A slight case of island fever. A common complaint, rarely fatal, though it can cause death – to ambition, and to energy, and to many things that seem so important and right in places less beautiful and in climates less clement.' He was gazing past Helen now, down to where swaying palms fringed a tiny bay, the waters of which glinted in the afternoon sun. Then he said softly, '"–the long-backed breakers croon, their ancient ocean legends to the lazy locked lagoon." And if you listen, and let yourself be drawn into the web of enchantment of sounds and scents – well then, there's no cure, no cure at all. You're bewitched, and there's no help.'

Helen was overwhelmed by an unexpected rush of sympathy for the handsome young man in his crumpled shirt, looking suddenly older than his years, and with despair in the droop of his shoulders. 'I read a poem called "The Lotus-Eaters" when I was at school,' she said quietly. 'It was about some sailors wrecked on a tropical isle. I can't remember much about it, but I know they gradually fell under the spell and didn't want to return home. I must read it again. I'll be able to understand it better now.'

'Oh, yes. Dear old Alfred, Lord Tennyson. I wonder what he knew about it. The bit I trotted out was Kipling. He had been around, though I doubt if he ever saw a locked lagoon. I never have. There is a small atoll just a mile or so to the south-west of Victoria that is an almost complete circle of coral. Over there.' He turned her so that she was looking in the direction he was indicating, and rested the other hand on her shoulder.

It seemed to Helen that they were the only people in the world, as she scanned the endless vista of blue. 'I can't see anything – except the ocean.'

'No, not from here. You can see the atoll from the mountain, but I'll do better than show you it. I'll take you across as soon as we can get a free day.'

'That won't be for quite a while, will it? It's nearly four months since the last nurse left, so there must be a lot of work for me to catch up on. I must–'

'You must not–' his arm around her shoulder tightened to emphasize each word, 'start talking about work already. There is always work, but there is also always time – especially in the islands. Now, as I was saying, I'll take you across to my atoll one day soon.'

She smiled and did not pursue the argument. Instead she asked the doctor if he had a boat, at which he threw back his head and laughed.

'A boat? Me? You must be joking, child. An impecunious medical dogsbody owning a boat! No, darling, I shall try to persuade our wealthy author to lend me his craft. You haven't met Mr Wakefield yet. Godfrey Wakefield. Ever heard of him?'

Helen shook her head. 'I don't think so. What sort of things does he write?'

'Oh, travelogue stuff, most of it is printed in American magazines,' he told her, making it obvious by the tone of his voice that he had no high opinion of the other man's work. 'He digs up odd bits of local history or folklore and lets his imagination run riot over them. Then he serves them up with a couple of highly-coloured, carefully-posed photographs and receives stacks of lovely dollars for them. Nice work if you can get it!' he finished.

'I don't suppose he was always so success-ful,' Helen said thoughtfully. 'Writers usually have to struggle for a long time before get-ting recognized.'

Colin Fraser shrugged. 'I wouldn't know about that. All I know is that he has far and away the finest house on the island, that he bought a new cabin cruiser a few weeks ago which must have set him back a packet and that, in general, he lives in a style to which a poverty-stricken young medico would give his eye teeth to become accustomed. My pay wouldn't keep his wife in nylons!'

'He's married, then?'

'He is, to the most beautiful woman I've ever seen, and that includes film and television stars.'

Helen made no comment on this, but noted to herself that however much her companion might admire the lady's beauty, he did not like her as a person. This opinion was confirmed when the doctor went on, 'Yes, Anna Wakefield is certainly lovely to look at. As flawless as a marble statue – and just as hard and cold.'

There was an uncomfortable silence for several moments, then Colin squeezed Helen's shoulder and laughed, looking down at her anxious young face. 'Don't look so worried, darling. I seem to be in one of my carping moods. You'll be meeting these people soon, and then you can make up your own mind about them. You mustn't let my ramblings weigh with you. Speak as you find, I always say. Come on, let's move on a bit further. It's twenty miles round the island and we haven't covered five yet.'

Helen smiled as they walked back to the car, but throughout the rest of the warm, golden afternoon, she could not shake off a slight feeling of apprehension. It seemed that in coming to this faraway island she had done more than take a new job; she had entered a strange new world filled with people very different from those simple folk among whom she had spent her life in dear, familiar Llandelly.

When they got back to the McFarlanes' bungalow, Colin Fraser said, 'I won't come in, Helen. I have things to do.' He got out of the car and came round to open the door for her.

Remaining where she was, she asked if there was anything she could do to help, adding, 'That is what I'm here for, and I'd like to start as soon as possible – meeting the people and learning about the work I'll be doing. At the moment I haven't much idea.'

'Bless the girl!' he appealed, raising his hands to the sky, 'Don't you ever think of anything but work?' He leaned towards her and said softly, 'There are other things, you know, things that ought not to be pushed into the background – especially by slender young maidens with golden hair and warm blue eyes.'

Helen was wondering, not for the first time that afternoon, whether the doctor had been drinking. His untidy appearance and the rather exaggerated way he expressed himself made it seem very likely. She had never in her life been addressed as 'Darling' on such short acquaintance, and – but even as she wondered, she acknowledged that it was possibly her own strict upbringing and background that made her interpret in this manner behaviour others would consider perfectly normal. She told herself she must keep an open mind, and not make the mistake of applying Llandelly's standards here. Victoria Island had its own code, and she must learn it and adapt herself to it.

She smiled and picked up her handbag and gloves from the dashboard compartment. 'If there's nothing I can do I may as well go and get some rest.'

'I hope you enjoyed the drive?' he asked, pushing back the white gate for her to go through. It swung creakily to between them.

'Yes, I did, thank you. Er – I will see you tomorrow morning, Doctor?'

He frowned. 'The eagerness to meet again I like, but why the formality, darling? The name is Colin, remember?'

'Yes. All right. When we're off duty,' she agreed, then asked determinedly, 'About tomorrow – you will have time to show me around a little? I'd like to see the hospital as soon as possible.'

'Hospital? Well, you could call it that I suppose, though it sounds a shade pretentious for a shack with half a dozen rickety beds in it.'

Helen watched him uncertainly as he delivered this scathing comment. Was he serious? Or was he teasing her? It was hard to decide for his face gave no clue.

'What did you expect on a tiny island in the middle of the Pacific Ocean?' he demanded. 'Guy's or Barts'? Because if you have any high-flown notions about white tiles and shining chromium, the sooner you forget them the better.'

'I haven't. I mean, I don't expect to find a – a large, well-equipped hospital such as I would in a city–'

'That's something,' he put in drily.

'–but I don't believe it's as bad as you say,'

she went on with a lift of her chin. 'You're trying to scare me.'

'Am I? Well, perhaps, a little. I can see I'm wasting my time, though, because you obviously have a lot in common with those fearless Welsh mountain ponies I've seen.'

'You know Wales?'

Her eager question amused him. 'Any other girl would have resented comparison with a horse. You take it as a compliment.'

'So it is. But you haven't told me which part of Wales you know. You aren't Welsh yourself?'

'I'm afraid not. I've spent holidays in Tenby, but you would probably say that the real Wales is the north.'

'Yes, that's true,' she said firmly.

He bowed deeply over her hand. 'I can only defer to your superior knowledge, Helen bach,' he murmured, then straightening up, he plucked a spray of blossom from a nearby frangipani tree. Milky liquid spurted from the broken stem and he shook it till the last drop fell. He tucked the bloom behind her ear, its crimson petals bright against her fair hair and skin. She put up a hand to remove it but he grasped her wrist. 'No, leave it. It looks delightful – and slightly incongruous. Rather like a child wearing her mother's high-heeled shoes.'

She was not sure what he meant by this, but left the flower where it was until, having said goodbye to Colin, she turned to walk up the path and saw that the McFarlanes were standing at the top of the steps. A wave of self-consciousness brought colour to her cheeks so that they almost matched the exotic blossom in her hair. 'Hello, I'm back!' she called to the waiting couple, and then on the pretext of bending to smell some shrubs bordering the path brushed the flower to the ground.

Gaining the verandah, she dropped her handbag and gloves on to a chair and took off her hat. 'I hope I haven't been too long,' she said to Mrs McFarlane, smiling apologetically.

The older woman smiled too, but only with her mouth. 'So long as you're here now, that's the main thing,' she replied, moving towards the hall door. 'I daresay you'll be ready for a bath by this?'

'Yes, please.' Helen followed her very stiff-backed hostess into the hall and through to her bedroom. It was a pleasant room with pretty flowered curtains and bedspread, though the furniture was old-fashioned and rather shabby.

Abstractedly rearranging the things on the mahogany dressing-table, Mrs McFarlane said, 'It's not very grand, but I hope you'll be comfortable.'

'I'm sure I will. It's a charming room,' Helen said warmly, 'and it's awfully kind of you to go to so much trouble–'

'No bother at all, ma dear.' The little Scotswoman came to take her hands tightly. 'We're happy to have you here, Angus and I, and we want you to regard this as your home. You'll need to forgive me if I fuss you sometimes. You see, we have a daughter just a wee bit older than yourself – Mary.' Tears began to well into her eyes and she blinked them away, smiling, 'Goodness me, what am I being so silly for? There's nothing to greet over. You young gels are so independent these days; you think nothing of going thousands of miles from everything you know, and taking up new ways of life.'

'Didn't you do that, when you left Scotland to come out here?'

'Och, that was different! I was married to Angus, and when he decided he wanted to work in the mission field I naturally came with him.' Helen asked if Mary was married.

'No, not yet. She's a teacher, but very much like her father, and soon after she left university she announced her intention of joining a group of graduates in starting a school in Peru. So that's where she is now, somewhere in the mountains near Lima among primitive tribes, some of them still as savage as they were centuries ago.'

Helen said: 'She must be very brave, and adventurous. Much more so than I am. I'm afraid I would never have thought of leaving home if I hadn't been practically pushed into it.' She explained about Mair and how it had come about that she had taken her friend's place in filling the vacancy on Victoria.

'So that was the way of it. I know my heart sank when I had to leave my cosy manse. I didn't consider sailing for the South Seas all that exciting, either.' Mrs McFarlane smiled, 'We've been happy though, and I'd be sorry to move now. Well, I mustn't stand chattering. I'll go and run your bath water.' At the door she turned to look at her young guest. 'I want your stay here to be happy too, Helen, and you must try to understand my feeling responsible for you. It's because of Mary.' Her voice trembled slightly and she bit her lip, then said quietly, 'I would like to be able to feel that there was someone keeping a motherly eye on my girl, but there isn't.

I can only pray God will take care of her.' She sniffed and searched in her pocket for a handkerchief: before she found it, a mischievous reflection lightened her face. 'Angus would be furious if he heard me say that and of course Mary could not be in better hands than God's but och! He has so many to watch over!' Locating a hankie, she blew her nose vigorously. 'Now I really am going. One of the maids unpacked your things. Perhaps you would have a look round and see they are where you want them. See you later on.'

Helen undressed and put on a thin blue housecoat. Then she sat at the dressing-table and started to brush her fair hair with long, thoughtful strokes. The face looking back at her from the mirror appeared exactly the same as if she had been in her bedroom at home in Llandelly, and this seemed strange. So much had happened so quickly after years of uneventful living that she did not feel the same girl as she had been – say, on the day Mair had come to her with the letter from the Medical Commission offering her the post of nurse to the people on Victoria Island, and had somehow persuaded Helen to take the job instead. Somehow. She was still not sure how her friend had accomplished this feat. Perhaps Colin Fraser had been right, and she was not as contented as she thought. Perhaps she had, without even being aware of it, wanted to widen her experience, to see what lay beyond her own small world and to find out how she would acquit herself in different surroundings and among different people.

Whatever the deep-seated motive behind her agreeing to come, here she was, and already she felt in some way more alive than before. She leaned a little nearer to the mirror. Surely she ought to be at least sun-tanned, if there was no other apparent change, but her skin was as fair as ever. She sighed. She had looked forward to acquiring a lovely golden tan for the first time in her life. Plenty of time, though.

She got up and began to glance through the drawers and wardrobe where her clothes had been arranged neatly. It was rapidly getting dark and before lighting the lamps she went to draw the curtains across the french window. Lights blazing out from a large house further up the hill attracted her attention and she wondered if the author Colin Fraser had mentioned lived there. What was his name? Wakefield. Godfrey Wakefield. That was it. And his wife was called Anna and was very beautiful.

Beyond the house, the jagged mountains rose black against the purple and scarlet sky, and Helen watched the colours melt into one another and deepen until she suddenly realized she was shivering. She closed the window and went gratefully to her warm bath.

Chapter Four

Dinner was served in the cool, candle-lit dining-room, and the Rev. Angus McFarlane was a cheerful host with many stories to tell of his years on the island. His wife, too, was more relaxed, the tension Helen had detected in her earlier having disappeared. Or at least the young nurse thought it had. When she began to talk about her afternoon drive, however, she noticed the older woman's lips tighten and the conversation flagged.

It was a relief to all three when a knock at the front door was followed by footsteps and voices in the passage. Mrs McFarlane jumped up.

'We asked our neighbours to pop in and meet you,' she told Helen. 'You don't mind, do you?'

The dining-room door was opened by a smiling, brown-skinned girl in a brightly-patterned sarong, who ushered in a strikingly handsome couple.

Helen looked at the guests with interest. The man was tall and distinguished, with

51

white hair. He looked to be about fifty; his white dinner jacket emphasized the deepness of his tan. The woman beside him was tall too, and as slim and graceful as a willow in her sheath-like dress of lime-green silk. Her hair was copper-bright and swathed her small head in a smooth coil. She was lovely, and Helen knew before the maid announced the visitors who they were.

'Mistah Godfrey Wakefield and his wife, ma'am,' the islander said carefully, then bobbed and stepped back into the doorway, grinning shyly.

'Thank you, Ria,' Mrs McFarlane smiled kindly at the girl. 'We'll have coffee in the other room in a few minutes,' she said, and when the maid had gone, turned to her guests. 'I'm so glad you could come.'

'Yes, indeed,' her husband agreed. 'Come and meet our new nurse – Miss Helen Davis. She arrived this afternoon. I – don't think I need to tell you where she hails from?'

'With a name like that she must be Welsh,' Godfrey Wakefield said without noticeable interest, and gave Helen's hand a brief clasp.

Anna Wakefield showed even less enthusiasm. She merely touched hands and murmured 'Hello', her cool green eyes taking note of the other's appearance in one sweeping glance. Helen thought, 'She's much younger than her husband; thirty at the most. And so beautiful.' Even at such close quarters there was no flaw in her creamy complexion or the sculptured perfection of her face and features.

Mrs McFarlane pushed aside a partition to reveal another room furnished with settees and easy chairs. Like the rest of the house this room was homely and comfortable, and the only concession to fashion was in the contemporary design of the material used for the cushions that brightened the dull browns of the upholstery and floor-coverings.

The hostess invited her guests to make themselves at home and they went through. The Wakefields sat on one settee, Helen and the host on the other facing them. Mrs McFarlane said: 'It's more cosy in here, isn't it?' and placed herself on a chair beside a low table between the settees.

Anna Wakefield, perching on the edge of her seat, crossed her long, slim legs and, watching her, it seemed to Helen that in this setting she was as out of place as a bird of paradise in the highlands of Scotland. Then she smiled to herself. Goodness, she was getting fanciful!

The young nurse leaned back, smoothing her skirt over her knees. She wished she had put on something more becoming than the sleeveless beige dress that she knew did nothing to enhance her delicate prettiness. Not that she could ever hope to compete with Mrs Wakefield for attraction whatever clothes they wore. 'I'm sorry–' she said, realizing that Godfrey Wakefield had spoken to her.

He smiled patiently. 'I merely enquired about your journey, Miss Davis. A hackneyed gambit, I would agree, but–' He shrugged elegantly, and drew on his cigarette.

'Oh, no, it's kind of you. I'm afraid my mind was wandering for a moment.'

'Not a bit of wonder,' Mrs McFarlane declared sympathetically. 'The poor wee gel must be worn out with one thing and another. She ought to have had a rest when she arrived,' she frowned and shook her head reproachfully at Helen, 'but instead of that she would go off exploring.'

Godfrey Wakefield's handsome head jerked up. 'So you have seen something of our island already, Miss Davis? How enterprising of you. What did you think of it?'

'Oh, it's beautiful!' Helen sat forward, her

eyes shining. 'The colours – the sea and the sky, the flowers, the mountains – they're so clear; and the air – it's so fresh and sweet with the scent of the blossom, and the breeze from the ocean.'

'You have quite a charming gift for words,' the writer told her, with a faintly patronizing smile, adding, 'but then you are Welsh, aren't you?' He stubbed out his cigarette in an ash-tray and then said, 'You know, you give the impression of being surprised to find Victoria Island a delightful place, and that in turn surprises me. Have the South Sea Islands no longer the hold they once had on men's dreams? When I left civilization twenty-five years ago I was the object of considerable envy. All my friends and acquaintances confessed a secret yearning to do the same thing. Of course, they would never take the plunge, but none of us had the least doubt that life on a Pacific island would be heaven on earth.' He regarded Helen for a moment through narrowed, pale eyes, before asking slowly, 'Why not you, I wonder?'

She looked down at her hands, embarrassed at being put on the spot in this way. 'Well – I don't really know. I suppose I thought the – the glamour of the islands was something unreal, built up by films and in books, where all the unpleasant aspects are ignored and the pleasing ones exaggerated out of recognition. And then– Oh, dear–' she stopped, her embarrassment increasing miserably as she realized what she had said. 'I'm sorry.' She forced herself to raise her eyes and look at the author, and repeated, 'I'm sorry. I didn't mean that you–'

'That I – distort the facts?' he interrupted haughtily. 'Hide truths that would be unpalatable to my readers? Paint a misleading picture to satisfy people who don't want their illusions shattered? Oh, but I do, my dear Miss Davis. I do. Is that wrong? I don't think so. I am not a reporter whose job it is to relate what he sees. I am a creative writer and as such I claim the freedom to decide for myself – with my public in mind – what is worth telling and what is better left out.'

The clergyman opposite leaped now to Helen's defence. 'Come now, Wakefield, I canna have my young guest badgered like this, particularly on her first day,' he reprimanded. 'She forgot your profession for a minute or she would not have made that remark–' he winked outrageously at Helen and muttered, 'however justified.'

'Now then, don't let us start that old argument,' Mrs McFarlane begged. 'Ah, good. Here's the coffee at last. Put it down, Ria. I'll pour.'

The native girl placed the laden tray carefully on the low table near her mistress and, with her usual bob, padded softly from the room.

Helen was grateful for the chance this diversion gave her to collect herself and, as she sipped her coffee, she stole a glance at Anna Wakefield to discover how that lady had taken the slight contretemps. Not unexpectedly, there was no sign of perturbation on the lovely impassive countenance of the author's wife.

Stirring his coffee, Godfrey Wakefield asked Helen how much of the island she had seen.

'Quite a lot,' she told him. 'We drove the whole way round the coast and Dr Fraser–' she faltered, noticing that this name did provoke immediate response from Anna Wakefield, who was staring at her now intently, her usually cool green eyes suddenly sparkling. 'Er – he stopped several times so that I could admire the view.' Helen's voice trailed off weakly under that intimidating glare.

Mrs Wakefield seemed to lose interest, but later, when she and Helen were alone for a few minutes, she returned to the subject of Colin Fraser. 'So you've met our doctor already, Miss Davis? What do you think of him?'

'I've only been here a few hours,' Helen said evasively.

The other woman raised dark brows. 'How wise you are to reserve judgment, because you have a lot to learn, believe me.' A lot to learn, Helen thought. That's what Colin had said to her. A cold shiver swept over her. She felt afraid of what lay behind these words.

Chapter Five

Knowing that days begin early in the Islands, Helen was ready at half-past seven next morning. Wearing one of the smart uniforms she had been issued with – short-sleeved white nylon dress and white shoes – she came out onto the verandah. Her fears of the previous evening seemed unreal in the bright morning sun.

She was still waiting an hour later when Mrs McFarlane, business-like in a grey two-piece, joined her. 'I thought you were being rather optimistic, getting prepared so early, Helen,' she said, sitting in a wicker chair opposite the young nurse.

'I thought he'd want me to help with his surgery.'

The Scotswoman said slowly: 'I shouldn't expect too much if I were you, dear. I mean, things won't be the same here as in your hospital, and I'm afraid you'll be disappointed if you imagine they will. It isn't easy to make you understand when you're so new to the ways of the island, but I wanted to warn –

no, no, to explain the difference you are bound to find.'

'I do understand, Meg,' Helen replied with a confident smile. She was surprised at her hostess making such an issue of this. 'Dr Fraser left me no illusions.'

But Mrs McFarlane did not appear to take comfort from this assurance. She said. 'Dr Fraser – yes – well, there you are. He is not quite like your doctors at home, is he?'

Helen got up and went to the verandah rail. She did not want to discuss Colin. Meg went on: 'It's living out here; it affects every-one, but if a person is already – easy-going – it's worse.'

Helen did not reply at once. She found herself resenting the implied criticism of Colin; resenting it bitterly, and she didn't want to betray her feelings if she could help it. 'It's still quite early,' she said evenly, when her indignation had cooled a little, 'and he might have been delayed in all sorts of ways. A call – something wrong with the car–'

'I'm sorry, ma dear.' Mrs McFarlane came to stand beside Helen and put a hand placat-ingly on her arm. 'I didn't mean to upset you. That's the last thing I would want. It's just that, as I told you last night, I feel responsible for you. Especially after what happened – oh!' she broke off suddenly in obvious confusion, and Helen frowned.

'What do you mean?'

'Oh, nothing really. I shouldn't have said that. I ought to have been more tactful.'

Helen's sympathy for her embarrassed hostess was tempered by her own still-keen resentment. 'I'd prefer honesty to tact,' she said stiffly. 'For some reason you dislike Dr Fraser and you want me to feel the same way. Well, I'm sorry. I know you're doing what you think is right, but I'm not a child and I shall make up my own mind.'

Both women turned as they heard the roar of an engine, and a second later, Colin Fraser's red sports car screeched to a halt at the gate. 'I don't know when I'll be back,' Helen said, and ran down the verandah steps.

'Take care, ma dear,' Meg called earnestly after the slight figure. Then she sighed. 'Angus was right, Jonah,' she said to the huge black cat that appeared from indoors to stretch himself luxuriously in the sun, 'he told me this would happen.'

'You look worried, darling,' Colin Fraser observed, taking his eyes briefly from the steeply climbing road they were driving up.

Helen smiled unconvincingly. 'No, I'm not worried.'

'Then why are you staring at your hands instead of looking at the scenery, which is usually considered worth a second glance? You haven't given it the first yet.'

The road wound its way around a mountain; on one side of it was rich, dense forest, on the other a view of the coast-line, pale sand meeting green water that merged into sapphire beyond the reef, groups of palms casting black shadows, a cluster of native huts nestling in a hollow. 'It's lovely,' she said, gazing about her, trying to appear more interested than she felt.

Her companion was not taken in. 'What's on your mind? Something is, so you can stop evading the issue.'

'It's nothing – nothing important. Just a little disagreement I had with Mrs McFarlane.'

'Oh?' Colin threw her a shrewd glance.

'I'm afraid I was awfully rude to her,' Helen went on miserably, 'and she's been so kind.'

Taking one hand briefly from the steering wheel to grip hers, Colin said, 'I can't imagine you being rude to anyone unless they thoroughly deserved it. And I know Meg

McFarlane. She's all right so long as you toe the line, that is, the line according to her; if you don't subscribe to her views and dare to say so, she can be as ruthless as anyone.' Again there was the bitterness in his voice that Helen had noticed the previous day when the subject of conversation had been the same. 'What was the argument about?'

She turned away so that he might not see the colour rise to her cheeks. But he did. 'So it was me,' he said flatly.

'In a way,' she admitted, 'but don't let's talk about it now. It's such a beautiful morning and the scenery is glorious, as you said. How much further is it to the hospital?'

'All right,' he laughed, 'I'll drop the subject, since the fact that you disagreed with our Meg proves you haven't let her influence you. I appreciate that, darling,' he added, giving her hand a squeeze. Then a tricky bend in the road claimed his attention for a few moments. 'Only another mile or so to go,' he told her when the going was level again.

'Isn't it inconvenient to have the hospital so far away from the villages?'

'I suppose it is, but the air is much cooler and cleaner.'

'Yes, of course. I can feel the difference.

This would be ideal for a sanatorium.'

'It is partly used for respiratory diseases.'

She looked at him, frowning slightly. 'The same building, you mean?'

'There is only one,' he pointed out, and her frown deepened.

'But surely–' she began, and then thought better of it. She must tread warily. Not try to do too much too quickly. Even on such short acquaintance she realized that if there were improvements to be made she would achieve more by gentle persuasion than by antagonizing Colin. 'Oh, what's that?' she asked as they turned a corner and a large hut came into sight. It had a corrugated iron roof; the window-spaces were draped with grubby netting, and the rough grass around it was so over-grown that it reached the level of the verandah.

'That,' said Colin, 'is it; the Queen Victoria Island General Hospital, the ditto Sanatorium, Mental Asylum and Leper Colony, all in one.' He drove on to the grass and stopped the car a few yards from the verandah steps. These were almost hidden by climbing vegetation and at one side Helen noticed a pile of refuse, partially concealed by a mass of exquisite gardenias. Was this typical of the whole island, she wondered.

Beauty and colour on the surface, thinly disguising a festering sore of poverty and ignorance.

They got out of the car and walked up to the verandah. Here two men lay sleeping on narrow beds in the shade. Their bodies were so undernourished that each rib was visible; their only clothing was the piece of cotton material each wore around his hips. Helen tried not to let her feelings show but, trained as she was to regard cleanliness as very close to Godliness, she couldn't help being shocked at such neglect. The patients appeared not to have been washed that morning and they had no bed covering whatever.

Silently, she accompanied the doctor into the gloomy building. There were six beds here, two of them occupied by wretched-looking elderly men. 'Malaria,' Colin muttered.

'I suppose that's the most common disease here?'

He nodded. 'There's not much we can do in the way of treatment but these old chaps are in such a low state due to malnutrition we're trying to build them up a bit.'

'The main thing with malaria is to get rid of the places where the mosquitoes live and breed and stamp it out that way, isn't it?'

Helen asked, casting her mind back to the brief and hurried cramming of such matters she had done before leaving Wales.

Colin nodded again. 'It's a splendid idea, but who's going to do it? The teams of bright young scientists the U.N.O. send to practically every corner of the earth haven't penetrated this far with their D.D.T. sprays and what-have-you—'

They had come out of the ward into a small room furnished with a table, two wooden chairs and a metal cabinet. After the experience of the past few minutes, Helen was pleasantly surprised to see a fitted wash-basin in one corner. Colin perched on the table and took out his cigarettes. Helen refused one, and he lit his own. What had things been like here while her predecessor was there, Helen was wondering. Obviously conditions had worsened during the months the hospital had been without a trained nurse. 'What about the rest of the staff?'

'The rest of the staff?' he repeated, pushing back his long, untidy brown hair. 'Oh, yes. I must introduce you to him.'

'Him?'

'Yes, Thomas Jones. His father was a compatriot of yours; a seaman who passed this way some twenty years ago – so his mother tells him. She's an Islander, of course. Thomas is a bright lad. He went to the mission school.'

Helen took her cap from the case she had brought and began to make it up. She felt a crisp white uniform was rather out of place, but she was there as a nurse and might as well look like one. As she pinned the cap into position, Colin watched her closely.

'Delightful,' he said, when she had finished, and reached for a white coat that hung behind the door and put it on, grinning sardonically. He clasped his hands behind him and stooped slightly in the time-honoured medical manner. 'Well, nurse, shall we continue our tour of inspection? The orthopaedic department next? Here we are–' and he bowed towards a dusty collection of splints and weights in a corner of the room. 'You'd like to see our laboratory? Certainly. There it is.' He pointed a languid hand at the top of the cabinet on which stood a rack of test-tubes and a microscope. 'Now what else–' He broke off and came to her, putting his hands on her shoulders. 'I'm sorry darling,' he said with a gentleness that contrasted strangely with his hard sarcasm of a moment ago.

She bit her lip, not looking at him. 'It – it's

all right.'

'No, it's not. It's all wrong.' He drew her to him, stroking her neck caressingly. 'I don't blame you for being disgusted with the whole set-up here.'

She raised her head then, her large blue eyes bright with tears. 'I didn't say that.'

'You didn't need to say it. You're not clever enough to hide your feelings. Those huge, clear eyes of yours will give you away every time.'

She flushed, turning her head away, and he laughed softly. 'What are you afraid I'll see there now?' he asked, his lips brushing her cheek. Embarrassed, she tried to step back but his arms held her tightly; then suddenly he let her go and she moved across to the door.

'Are there any more patients?' she asked steadily.

He shook his head. 'Not at the moment.'

'Is that because the people on the island are in good health, or because they don't come to the hospital when they are ill?'

Her question made him become serious again. 'Shrewd, aren't you, my love?'

'I just wondered if the islanders are suspicious or prejudiced against things they don't understand. I mean, it would be natural enough,' she explained quickly, in an attempt to gloss over any implied criticism of himself he might have suspected lay behind her query.

'Of course it would,' he agreed, 'but, natural or not, prejudice and suspicion ought to be broken down. There was plenty of those when anaesthetics were first discovered; they were overcome then and could be again, here, but – oh, Lord! I'm no fighter!' He dropped dispiritedly into a chair, stretching out his long legs and pushing his hands into the pockets of his coat.

Helen, standing with one hand on the door-handle, didn't know what to do or say. She felt sympathy for the young doctor and wanted to help him, but was afraid to show her concern for the disturbing effect his touch had upon her was still very much on her mind, and she knew it would be wise to avoid getting closely involved with this attractive man. 'I'm sure you've done your best,' she said eventually.

'Thanks, darling, for those few kind words.' He looked up at her with a wry expression and spread out his hands in a gesture that took in the room they were in and the ward beyond. 'If this is the best I'm capable of, I deserve to be struck off the

Register,' he growled. Then he shrugged and sighed deeply. 'Oh, I know it's a disgrace to the entire medical profession, this travesty of a hospital. I've always known it, but today I'm seeing it through your eyes and it's a grim experience I can tell you.' He brushed a hand across his eyes as if to wipe away the distasteful picture.

Helen's heart ached for him. 'You mustn't blame yourself so much,' she said. 'It's too big a job for one man to take on; – you haven't had even a trained nurse to help you for several months.'

He smiled and got to his feet. 'I love that soft Welsh lilt that comes into your voice sometimes. There's sweet you are, Helen bach,' he added, with a grossly exaggerated accent. Then more seriously, 'I mean it. You are sweet to try to comfort me.' He touched her cheek with his finger, and she drew in her breath sharply.

'Well, there's no sense in worrying about the past, is there?' Her voice was ridiculously shaky and she hoped this would pass unnoticed. 'The thing to do is to think how we can improve matters, isn't it? Now, er–' she moved away from him as casually as she could, 'you haven't shown me everything yet.'

'Do you want to see the wash-house and kitchen?'

'Yes, I do, but I meant the theatre. I haven't seen where you perform operations.'

'And you won't!' he told her harshly. 'There is no operating theatre. I am not considered capable of even the most elementary surgery, and if some people had their way I wouldn't be allowed to bandage a cut finger!'

'That's dreadful! What happens when an operation is needed?'

'If the patient can travel he goes to one of the bigger islands where they have proper facilities; if not, a doctor comes here with a portable theatre. We have a radio station here so we can contact Prince Albert Island – they run a sort of flying doctor service.'

'Is that necessary? I mean, couldn't you operate if you had the equipment?'

'Of course I could. But I told you, the powers-that-be have decreed that I am not to be trusted with a knife!'

'Who do you mean? The Medical Commission?'

'No, not them. They wouldn't have given me the job if they hadn't been satisfied I could deal with anything that cropped up. No, it's His Highness Dr Paul Strang who made the decision!'

Paul Strang. The name was familiar. Helen had a recollection of seeing this signature scrawled on one of the letters she had received regarding her appointment. 'He's the Medical Officer of Health, isn't he?'

'Yes, to the Royalty Islands. Medical Officer to a rather insignificant group of volcanic bits of rock somewhere in the middle of the Pacific,' he sneered. 'From the airs he gives himself you'd think he was God Almighty!'

'How unfair! You ought not to let him push you around.' Helen didn't often get angry, but this apparent injustice made her blood boil.

'I know. I keep on resolving to assert myself, but–' he shrugged helplessly, 'what's the use? He's the blue-eyed boy; he can do no wrong. I can't do a thing right.'

Helen went to him and laid a hand on his arm. 'Don't get depressed, Colin, please,' she pleaded quietly. 'Things will be better from now on, you'll see. We'll work together.'

He smiled down at her. 'Bless you, darling. I think I'm going to enjoy working with you. Oh, Helen!–' he pulled her roughly to him and held her so tightly that she gasped for breath, 'I needed you. I needed you so much. It will be better now, as you say. With you beside me, I'll be able to do all the things I've meant to do but just haven't got around to. You won't let me down, will you? You'll be loyal and reliable – like one of those Welsh mountain ponies I compared you with before.'

'I'll – do all I can – to help. That's what I'm here for,' she said breathlessly. She was struggling to keep calm; to hold back the tide of emotion that threatened to sweep over her. This was new; something she had never felt in her life, this tremendously powerful attraction for someone. No man she had ever met had had anything like this effect upon her. The few boy-friends she had had in Wales were young men she had known most of her life, gone to school and chapel with. Now she had met someone entirely different, and her reaction disturbed her. She clenched her hands hard. Told herself she was a nurse, that was why she was there, and she had work to do. A lot of work. 'Work,' she echoed, pushing him away, 'must get on.'

'Plenty of time,' he whispered against her hair.

'No, there isn't. There's lost time to be made up for before we begin to get anywhere.' She twisted out of his embrace and straightened her cap. 'Now – where will we find Thomas er – what's his name? – Jones, do you suppose? We must get some women in as soon as possible to give the place a thorough cleaning, and the garden must be attended to; it isn't healthy the way it is. Do you think we could possibly find somewhere else for the patients to stay for a day or two while the worst of the upheaval gets over? And–'

'Stop!' Colin clapped his hands to his temples. 'Please, darling, have pity!'

She looked at him, puzzled. 'I'm sorry. I was just–'

'Yes, I know. I agree with everything you say. One thing at a time, though. That's all I ask!'

When Helen walked up the path to the McFarlanes' bungalow late that afternoon, she was so tired she could think of nothing but how wonderful it would be to get into a warm bath and lie in it, completely relaxed, while the weariness seeped gradually from her body and the confusion resolved itself into some sort of order in her mind. It had been such an eventful, upsetting, exciting day. She had quite forgotten the quarrel between herself and her hostess; so much had happened since.

She remembered, though, when Mrs Mc-Farlane came on to the verandah. Helen hesitated at the foot of the steps until the older woman ran to join her, smiling, and put an arm through hers, saying sympathetically, 'You must be exhausted, ma poor lamb. Come away inside now. You'll be ready for a bath, I daresay, and it's ready for you. I ran it as soon as I heard the car.'

Leaving Helen at the bathroom door, she said, 'There'll be a meal ready whenever you are, so if you want to soak for a while, do so.'

She really was a kindly woman, Helen thought, as she took off the once-immaculate uniform. Now it was grubby and there was a tear in the sleeve. Oh, the warm scented water felt wonderful. Yes, it would have been awkward if Mrs McFarlane had taken offence over their difference of opinion. Would it be better to apologize or to let the matter drop? The Scotswoman didn't like Colin. Well, that was understandable. She no doubt considered him too young and irresponsible for the position he held. Perhaps in a way she was right. Colin was the type of person who worked well in partnership with someone possessing the practical qualities he lacked, but had not the self-discipline to work alone. Thus, after knowing him for less than forty-eight hours, did Helen sum up the character of Colin Fraser.

Chapter Six

If Helen was tired after her first day at the hospital, she was exhausted when the end of a fortnight came. There had been so much to do; but that had not been the hardest part. Getting down on her knees and scrubbing floors was much easier than trying to get any of the island folk to help. They were friendly and respectful when, with Thomas Jones acting as interpreter, she tried to explain the rudiments of hygiene, but their idea of cleanliness was very far removed from hers and as soon as her back was turned even their half-hearted efforts ceased. Mrs McFarlane had told Helen of two village women she thought might be suitable and Colin had driven them up to the hospital.

Of the four patients, Helen discovered that two were cured leprosy cases; cured, though the deformities the disease had caused would always remain. The only reason they were still in the hospital was that their families and former neighbours refused to accept them back into their communities, not understanding that modern science had taken much of the horror out of this ancient scourge. From centuries past, leprosy had been dreaded, its victims shunned as unclean, and this deep-seated belief would not easily be eradicated. So the two men had nowhere to go; the hospital was their only home.

Helen was troubled by this state of affairs. It was tragic that the wonderful blessing of a cure should be marred in this way. She could not hope to put this right, yet, if ever, but she could do something to improve the men's aimless existence and also get a much-needed job of work done – if her plan came off. She told them, again through Thomas, that they were no longer patients. From now on they were gardeners. They had to build themselves a separate hut to live in, and then they must clear the ground surrounding the hospital. As it was now, it was a breeding ground for germs and insects which caused and spread sickness.

The men hooked blank. Helen turned to Thomas.

'You pay, miss?' the half-caste asked. 'For English cigarette dey work.'

She nodded. 'Tell them they'll get five cigarettes each day if they work hard.'

This brought wide grins to the men's thin faces, and they went off happily to collect hibiscus stems for the walls of their hut. They could not be called keen workers, but with a strong incentive the job did get done.

Meanwhile the inside of the hospital was dealt with – after the scrubbing, everything was washed in antiseptic solution; netting over the windows was replaced with new material, uneven bed legs were straightened and such linen as there was well laundered. When Mrs McFarlane learned of the desperate shortage of supplies, she immediately promised to organize her women friends into a support group. They would turn out their own linen chests to see what they could spare, and also run some fundraising effort to provide amenities for the patients.

Helen found Thomas Jones invaluable. He was intelligent, and while he had inherited a cheerful disposition and a tendency to live in the present from his island mother, his Welsh father had endowed him with a brisk energy more usually found in colder climes. He had picked up a good knowledge of English and had learned quite a lot about medicine and nursing during the years he had worked at the hospital. He was rather inclined to stand on his dignity; he liked to be treated with the respect he considered his education and position entitled him, and he had not taken very kindly to Helen's demands. After a little coaxing though, and a little subtle flattery, he was persuaded that to wield a hammer or scrubbing brush was as important as any other task.

Colin had spent a good deal of time at the hospital, but had patients in various parts of the island and Helen insisted that he must not neglect these. At the end of the second week he came to take her home and found her in the office, painting out the medicine cupboard. He took the brush from her and laid it across the tin of paint. Then he put his hands on her shoulders and looked closely at her. Her face was pale, her hair untidy and smeared here and there with white paint from the hand she kept pushing it back with, and there were shadows under her eyes making them appear larger and darker than usual.

'You're worn out, my poor sweet,' he said tenderly, and kissed her forehead lightly.

'I am a bit tired, but the worst's done now. Tomorrow–'

'Tomorrow,' he put in firmly, 'is your day off.'

'Oh, no. I can't take a day off just now,' she replied with equal firmness. 'Perhaps when everything's going smoothly–'

'When everything's going smoothly you'll be ready for a hospital bed yourself.'

She smiled and shook her head. 'What rubbish! I'm fine.'

'You're worn out, as I said,' he persisted. 'If you go on flogging yourself like this, you'll collapse, and then you'll have to rest. Not for a day or two either. You'll be out of action for months. So you see, Nurse Davis,' he rubbed his forehead against hers, his voice gentle now, 'you are being very selfish if you refuse to obey my order. I'm not sure it isn't insubordination, as well.'

'There's so much to do–'

'And so much time, darling. I've told you before, life goes at a slower pace in the islands. You must try to adapt to it or you'll be banging your head against a brick wall, and,' he added gallantly, 'it's much too pretty for that.'

She sighed. 'I suppose you're right.'

'Of course I am. In fact, pretty is too mild a word. You're–'

'Silly!' she laughed, 'I didn't mean that! I meant about not rushing my fences. I suppose Thomas could keep an eye on things here for one day. He's very good.'

'That's settled then. C'mon now. I'll take you home.'

She took off her cap and went to the wash-basin. 'I think I'll go and see Meg's school tomorrow,' she said. 'I promised to go the first opportunity I got.'

'You haven't got the opportunity now,' he retorted, and as they walked out to the car he explained that he had borrowed Godfrey Wakefield's boat and was going to take her out to the nearby atoll he had told her about on her first day on the island. 'It'll be perfect. Just you and me. We'll take some food and wine and have a marvellous day of swimming and sun-bathing and lazing around away from everyone and everything but us.'

She got into the car. 'It sounds – nice,' she said weakly.

'It will be wonderful,' he replied, getting in beside her.

It was, too. At least, it was for most of that clear, bright May day. The warm sun sparkled on the white superstructure of the borrowed cabin cruiser and shimmered on the calm ocean, and Helen stood at the rail watching the gulf widen between boat and island. She was wearing a full-skirted blue dress with separate tiny jacket and a matching bandeau to keep her hair tidy. She resolved to relax and enjoy this break, to forget the hospital for a while. Thomas had had no qualms when she had rung him up earlier that morning to tell him that, if all was well, he was to take charge; in fact, he had greeted the prospect with smug delight. So there was nothing to mar the serene happiness of the day.

Soon Colin was pointing out to her a broken circle of pinky-grey coral jutting through the water ahead. 'That's it!' he said excitedly. 'My atoll. Almost a complete ring of coral. The highest point is only twelve feet above sea level, but when you're inside the lagoon you're in another world.' His voice was dreamy now, his eyes half-closed and fixed on the goal they were rapidly approaching. 'A refuge from all the worries and interferences of the outside world.'

Helen smiled sympathetically, but wondered a little that his mind should run on such lines. He seemed to sense what she was thinking.

'You don't understand, do you? You've never found the world hostile in your young life. You've never felt the desperate urge to escape. I have, and when I feel like that I come here. We'll be in the lagoon in a couple of minutes and you'll see what I mean.'

He concentrated on steering towards a narrow gap in the coral, and then they were through. He stopped the engine and the boat glided silently except for the soft swish as it cut through the water and came to a stop on silvery white sand.

Looking around, Helen could indeed see why this had become a desirable haven to Colin when, as apparently sometimes happened, life was trying. The world seemed very far from this lovely quiet spot, coloured in turquoise and white, deep green and pink. 'It's very peaceful,' she said.

He nodded. 'It's very heaven.'

They smiled contentedly at each other, then he said, 'Better take your sandals off; we'll get our feet wet when we jump down.'

So, barefoot and hand in hand, they leapt into the shallow water and ran up the beach to drop, laughing, to the sand beneath a cluster of pandanus palms. Helen put the picnic basket into the shade after taking out a bottle of suntan oil. She took off her jacket and rubbed her arms and shoulders with the oil. Today she really would get a proper suntan.

They swam and sun-bathed their swimsuits dry, and searched for tiny hermit crabs, and climbed the miniature coral mountains to survey their private kingdom as it lay basking in the sun.

Then, feeling hungry, they opened the picnic basket. Helen had brought a cooked chicken and some crisp bread buns, Colin produced two bottles of red wine. 'I'll introduce you to some of the local dishes one day soon,' he promised, kneeling to pour wine into two goblets. 'Curried goat is good, and prawns in lime juice. And I'll show you how to build a native oven that'll beat any gas or electric machine in the world.'

'This isn't bad,' Helen said blissfully, leaning back against a palm tree, a chicken leg in one hand and a hunk of bread in the other.

Colin sat beside her, his muscular brown legs stretched out next to her slim pale ones. He wore only a pair of fawn cotton shorts; she had put her blue dress on over her swimsuit, and each time his bare shoulder brushed hers she felt a thrill tingling through her whole body.

They finished their meal with plump pink bananas, and Colin refilled their glasses. 'A toast!' he announced, raising his drink aloft, 'to Welsh Wales – may its sons – and more especially its daughters! – prosper in whatever far-flung corner of the earth their venturing spirit places them.'

'Cymru Am Byth!' Helen responded fervently, clinking her goblet against his before taking a long drink of the refreshing wine. And then in a quiet voice she said, 'Now let's drink to those with no venturing spirit who still somehow find themselves in far-flung corners of the earth, and spend half their time wondering how it happened.'

He looked thoughtful for a moment. 'I'll drink to that only if you'll add the amendment – but being glad it did. Oh, darling–' he threw down his glass and pulled her to him, 'I love you. I love you so much!'

Chapter Seven

In that idyllic setting, doubts and difficulties had no place; no reality. Only the warmth of the sun and the beauty of the surroundings had meaning; these, and the pulsing of her blood in response to the man holding her in his arms. 'Being – very glad it did, Colin,' Helen whispered.

He kissed her lips hard. 'Darling, I'm glad, too; so terribly glad you came into my life. You've made it seem worth living. Given me hope.' He rained kisses on her hair and her face and her throat, murmuring jerkily, 'You're so sweet – and gentle – Helen – oh, Helen–'

Breathless and slightly dazed, she pushed him away. 'Please, Colin, I – can't breathe.'

'Sorry, darling,' he said, and suddenly let her go, so that she fell backwards on to the sand. He bent over her, laughing. 'That was mean of me, wasn't it? Forgive? Say you do or I'll – I'll throw myself from the highest peak yonder,' he threatened dramatically.

She giggled. 'It's only a few feet high.'

'Heartless creature!'

'Hard as nails. Now go away. You're keeping the sun off me, and I want to get a tan.'

He didn't move, except to push aside one of the shoulder straps of her dress. Her hand went up quickly to replace it but was caught in his. 'You're getting one already, if that's what you want, though I think you're crazy to scorch that lovely fair skin. I can see where your strap's been. It'll look silly if you wear a strapless dress.'

'I never wear strapless dresses.'

'Oh, no. Of course you wouldn't dream of such a thing,' he replied with mock solemnity, 'not respectable, look you! And any girl who wore those fripperies would be no better that she should be, isn't it?'

Helen could not help laughing at his ridiculous accent, though she was feeling too disturbed to be really amused. 'I've never heard anyone say "look you" in my life except on the wireless,' she said stiffly.

'There's cruel you are, shattering my illusions!'

'I told you, I'm as hard as nails.'

'So you did.' He traced the white line of untanned flesh on her shoulder. She knew he was watching her closely, and avoided his eyes lest he should read in them the effect his touch had on her.

She felt more and more drawn to this so-different young man. She wanted him to take her in his arms again more than she had ever wanted anything. The strength of her desire shocked her. This was wrong, and all the force of her strict Welsh upbringing reminded her that it was. Swiftly, before her resolution failed, she turned on her side and jumped up.

She ran to the water, throwing off her dress as she went, and plunged into its cool depths. After a moment or two, she turned and looked back at the beach. Colin was standing, his long legs astride, watching her, shading his eyes against the strong sun. She waved and, after a brief pause, he waved back and ran to the water's edge. Soon he was beside her, splashing her playfully and laughing at her efforts to retaliate.

As the sun began to sink and lose a little of its power she ran back on to the sand and wrapped herself in her huge towel. 'Time we were thinking of getting back,' she told Colin when he joined her. 'I don't want Meg to be worried.'

He took one end of her towel and started rubbing her hair energetically with it. 'Why should she worry? Doesn't she think I can take care of you for a few hours?'

'It's not that,' Helen said evasively. It was, though. Meg had not been at all happy about this trip, though she had not said very much. For some reason the Scotswoman disapproved of Colin and of Helen's friendship with him; what the reason was remained a mystery to the young nurse. She could only guess that they were such completely different people that understanding between them was impossible. 'I – said I wouldn't be late,' she added lamely.

'It's the middle of the afternoon yet, darling. Forget about Meg. Forget about everybody but me.' His arms closed tightly around her and the towel fell to the ground. His body was warm and hard against her and the tang of salt water was on his lips as they met hers in passion. A moment later, without knowing how it happened, she was lying on the sand holding him to her and murmuring inarticulately of the feelings – strange, wonderful, heady feelings – that swept over her with tremendous force.

He raised his head a little. 'You're adorable,' he whispered, and kissed her throat and then the soft flesh of her breast, caressing her with urgent touch.

'Oh, Colin–' Her eyes closed.

Then, suddenly – 'No!' she cried, and fought desperately to free herself. She scrambled to her feet and ran, panting as she tried to hurry through the sand, knowing there was nowhere to run to, but unable to stop until she was exhausted and could not go any further.

She sat on a rocky ledge and put her head in her hands, sobbing quietly and uncontrollably.

When Colin came, he sat beside her but did not touch her. He did not speak until her sobs died away and she wiped her eyes with the back of her hand. She blinked, looking straight ahead, and he said in a flat voice unlike his own, 'What was all that about?'

She opened her mouth but no sound came and she just shook her head.

'Did I suddenly become so disgusting to you? So horrible that you had to get away from me?'

'No.' She began to weep again quietly. 'I – I'm sorry.'

He moved nearer and took her hand. She flinched. 'It's all right,' he said tenderly, 'don't be frightened. I'm not such a monster that I would force my unwelcome attentions on a girl – especially a strictly-brought-up girl from North Wales.'

'I don't see that it matters – where I come from,' she sniffed.

'Ah, but it does.' He looked at her now and she realized she must look a mess with her hair still damp from the sea and her eyes red with crying. He went on, 'I understand you so well, Helen; better than you understand yourself.'

'That's possible,' she muttered. 'I don't understand myself at all sometimes.'

He raised her hand to his lips. 'You don't know why you ran away from me just now. But I know.'

'Oh.' She glanced at him briefly and then turned away. 'It's time we were going,' she said unsteadily, and stood up.

He got up too keeping hold of her hand. 'You ran because you wanted me. You wanted me to make love to you. Didn't you? Admit it.'

'You're hurting me,' she quavered, and he relaxed his grip on her hand.

'I'm sorry, darling. I don't want to hurt you. I love you too much for that. You love me, too, don't you? Say you do.'

'Please, Colin – let's go now,' she asked, her blue eyes full of entreaty.

He sighed and then grinned. 'O.K. honey.

I know when I'm beaten.'

They were on their knees packing the picnic things into the basket when they heard the sound of an engine and a moment later a motor cruiser skimmed into the lagoon.

'Who the–' Colin jumped up, shading his eyes with his hand to stare at the newcomer. 'It looks like – but it can't be. He isn't due.'

Helen stood up too, and followed the direction of his gaze. Whoever it was Colin had in mind, there was no mistaking his displeasure at the unexpected arrival. 'Who is it, do you think?'

'I don't think now. I know,' he replied angrily. He was standing with his hands on his hips, watching as the boat beached and a man leapt down and strode towards them.

This man was not particularly tall, yet there was an air of effortless authority about him. He was lean, and his white shirt and trousers emphasized the tan of his skin and the blackness of his thick hair. He was not handsome, but his face was strong and his dark eyes direct and unwavering as they settled first on Helen and then on Colin. When he was within a couple of yards of them he stopped.

Colin said: 'This is a surprise, Strang. I

wasn't expecting you till the end of the month.' He turned to Helen. 'This is Dr Paul Strang.' Then to the other man, 'Nurse Helen Davis.'

'How do you do, Doctor?' She held out a rather grubby hand and it was taken in a firm grip. What awful luck, to meet her employer under these circumstances, she thought, painfully aware that in her crumpled swimsuit and with unkempt hair she appeared very different from the efficient, neat and self-possessed nurse she would have wished to look on this occasion.

'I wasn't too busy, so I made the trip to Victoria ahead of schedule to make your acquaintance, nurse. You arrived about two weeks ago, I believe? I went to the hospital, then to the McFarlanes'–'

'I'm sorry, Doctor,' Helen broke in apologetically. 'If I'd had any idea–'

Colin interrupted: 'She's entitled to a day off, isn't she?'

The other man ignored him coolly and completely. 'You couldn't know, of course,' he told Helen. 'I could see from the hospital that you have not been wasting your time since you got here – but we can talk about that another time. I don't want to spoil your off-duty. I would not have come except that Mrs McFarlane was rather anxious about you.'

'Meg? Anxious?' she asked, puzzled.

He nodded. 'Apparently you said you would be back early, and when it got around to six o'clock–'

'Six o'clock!' Helen was astonished. 'Goodness, I never dreamed it was so late. I left my watch on the boat.'

'It doesn't matter so long as you are all right.'

Colin stepped forward and demanded aggressively, 'Why shouldn't she be all right, for God's sake?'

Strang regarded him coldly and Helen said quickly, 'We were packing up when you came anyway, Doctor.' She shivered slightly. 'It's getting chilly.' She knelt down and hastily put the remaining picnic things into the basket, then folded the tea-cloth.

'I'll be pushing off then.' After a brief questioning glance at Helen, Paul Strang raised a hand. 'See you later. The Wakefields have invited us all to dinner.' Then he turned on his heel and stalked off.

'Bombastic devil!' growled Colin.

'Sh – he'll hear you.'

'Who cares? Why did he have to come

butting in here? I thought this was one spot where I could have some peace.' He dropped on to the sand and rested his chin sullenly on his knees. 'And he always has such a superior blasted attitude! Treats me as if I were unworthy of breathing the same air! God, it makes me wild!'

Helen looked at him sympathetically. 'Don't get upset. He probably doesn't mean to be like that. Some people just have an unfortunate manner.'

As if he hadn't heard her, he went on muttering, 'Damned prig that he is. He's a good match for Meg McFarlane. Anyone who dares to be an individualist instead of bending the knee to their sacred cows is beyond the pale.'

She sighed. It was getting quite cold. She put on her dress and jacket, then, wrapping her arms around herself in an effort to get warm, suggested that they might make a move.

He looked up at her then. 'Why? Because His Majesty Paul Strang thinks it's time we were back in the fold with all the other sheep? Are you going to be yet another conformist? If so, I'm disappointed, Helen. I thought I saw signs of an independent spirit in you.'

'It's nothing to do with Dr Strang or anyone else,' she replied a trifle sharply. 'I want to get home because I'm frozen.'

'Oh, darling, I'm so sorry!' He jumped up and put his arms comfortingly around her, his cheek against her hair. 'I am a selfish brute. Of course you'll be feeling the cold. I should have realized. Come along, then–' He picked up the basket in one hand and with the other still round her waist they ran to the boat.

Soon they were back on Victoria. The island looked different now with the quick tropical darkness falling subduing the colours of the bright day. Somewhere, someone was playing a haunting tune on a stringed instrument, and as they walked along the wooden jetty, a fragrant breeze caught their hair. At the end of the jetty Colin said to Helen, 'Wait here and I'll get the car.'

While he was gone, she stood looking across the still water. She couldn't see the atoll but pictured it, deserted again, with no-one to disturb its tranquillity.

Suddenly, she was aware of someone behind her and turned. 'Colin?' But he was not in sight. At first she could see nobody. Then a movement of the branches of a nearby frangipani tree attracted her attention. Nervously she took a step forward. There was only water behind so it was no use retreating. Another step, and she could dimly make out the figure of a girl half-hidden by the tree. Relieved, she approached and saw that the girl was wearing a boldly-patterned *pareu* and had a gardenia in her silky long black hair, and that she was beautiful in a way that owed everything to nature. Helen smiled. 'Hello. Is anything wrong? I'm a nurse.'

The native girl glared at her in hostile silence and then backed away and disappeared into the night.

Chapter Eight

This strange incident troubled Helen on the drive home, but when they reached the bungalow it slipped from her mind. Colin left her rather unceremoniously at the front gate and drove off, saying he would call for her later if she wanted to go to the Wakefields' dinner party. He obviously did not. Helen, although she would have much preferred to go to bed early, said she did want to go. A smart dinner party was the last thing in the world she was in the mood for. Nevertheless, she felt she must make the effort. There was a lot to do on the island and Paul Strang was the man to get it done. He had the authority. What she had to do was to make him see what needed doing, and before anything could be accomplished she must get on good terms with him.

More important, the antagonism between the two doctors must be broken down if they were to work together; and they had to work together for the sake of the islanders.

She went to her bedroom, hoping to avoid

Meg for a while, but her hostess was there drawing the curtains. Turning to look at the slightly-bedraggled girl, her face softened.

'Ma poor wee lass, you're like something Jonah might have dragged in,' she commiserated.

'That's just how I feel, except that your proud cat wouldn't lower himself to drag such a pathetic object as me for a yard,' Helen said. Then, hesitantly, she added, 'I'm sorry – about being late. I didn't realize – time seemed to slip by–'

The Scotswoman patted her hand. 'That's all right, dear. We won't fret about that the now. I've got your bath running, so come away and get out of that creased frock. I scarcely recognize ye.'

An hour later, Helen had contrived to transform herself from an untidy urchin into something more like herself. Her newly-washed hair shone; it was almost silver now from the effect of the strong sun, and the white sleeveless dress she wore emphasized the delicate tan she had acquired. Deep pink lipstick was the only make-up she used that evening.

She waited on the balcony until Colin arrived and then went down to meet him at the gate. Instead of commenting on her appearance as she expected, he asked if everything was all right.

'All right?' she queried. 'I think so. Why do you ask?'

He shrugged. 'Oh, I just wondered – what did Meg say when you got in?'

'Nothing much.' She smiled. 'She probably had a lot of things she meant to say, but when she saw me looking like something the cat dragged in, her maternal feelings got the better of her. She really is sweet.'

'Huh!' Colin snorted, opening the car door.

When they were well away from the bungalow, he said almost under his breath, 'So she didn't say anything much– That means she's saving it all up for a more convenient time.'

'Oh, I don't think so. All she was concerned about was whether there'd been an accident or something. It's natural that she should be over-anxious about me–'

'Why?' he rapped out, taking his eyes off the road to look at her and causing the car to swerve dangerously. 'Damn!' He righted it, drove on for a minute or two in silence, and then pulled in to the side of the road and stopped.

The silence was complete then, until Helen asked what was the matter. He was angry about something but she had no idea what it was. He said: 'I just want to know what you meant by that. Why should Meg McFarlane be over-anxious about you when you're with me?'

'I didn't say that,' she protested. 'I meant she worries more than she would if she hadn't a daughter of her own in a strange country. That makes her more inclined to mother me.'

'Oh – I see.' He was calmer now, but Helen was not.

'What did you think I meant?' she queried.

He shrugged. 'It doesn't matter.' He put an arm round her shoulders and drew her towards him. 'I haven't told you yet how delightful you look tonight,' he whispered, and kissed her cheek.

'No, you haven't,' she agreed with a smile.

'Well, you look delightful tonight, darling.'

'Thank you, sir.'

They laughed together, and Helen wondered that a man could change so swiftly from mood to mood. She had never known anyone like him. The few young men she had known in Wales had been so different – predictable, even-tempered. Perhaps that was why she had found them a bit uninteresting. Thinking of this made her feel homesick – a feeling that had never been far from the surface of her mind since she left Llandelly, and she clung to Colin when he kissed her again.

'Well, well!' he murmured, 'such hidden depths!' A moment later he stroked her hair and said, 'Let's scrub this dinner party. I know much better things to do on a starlit night than sit around making stilted conversation with stolid people.'

She sat back and patted her hair into place. 'Oh, I think we ought to go,' she said as firmly as she could when her heart was beating so much faster than normally.

He tried to change her mind but she would not be persuaded and, with a sigh, he gave in.

When they arrived at the Wakefields' elegant home they were shown through to the back verandah where half-a dozen people were having drinks. The hostess came towards them, soignée in black with diamonds. She smiled coolly and said, 'We were beginning to wonder if you were going to let us down. What will you drink?'

'Oh – sherry, please,' Helen said, and apologised for being late.

'Please don't worry about it. Dr Strang

has been telling us how frightfully hard you've been working since you came to Victoria.'

Looking past Anna Wakefield, Helen saw Paul Strang leaning against the verandah rail talking to an elderly couple she had never met.

Anna introduced them to her as Col. and Mrs Scott and then took Paul Strang away to show him some carved figure she had recently added to the collection she was apparently very proud of.

Helen chatted for a few minutes with her new acquaintances – they had retired to the island when the Colonel's army service was over – but when she caught sight of Colin standing beside the drinks trolley she found it difficult to keep her mind on the conversation. He was flushed, as if he had already had a fair amount of alcohol. Oh dear, she must stop him. It would spoil everything if he got drunk.

As soon as she could, she excused herself and went across to him. He was pouring out whisky and his hand was unsteady. 'Don't drink any more before dinner, Colin, please,' she said.

'Why not?' he replied truculently. 'That's the only reason I came. There's always plenty of booze here. Good stuff, too. There must be money in those corny yarns Wakefield churns out!'

'Sh – they'll hear you!'

'Who cares?'

At this moment, fortunately, a young island servant announced that dinner was served.

After the meal, the Scotts, Godfrey Wakefield and the other guest, a plain young woman who, Helen learned, was a sculptress, stayed indoors to play bridge. The others returned to the verandah.

Colin loosened his tie and dropped into a low chair beside the drinks. Paul Strang frowned disapprovingly at him and then strolled away to stand at the top of the steps looking pensively out across the garden. Helen hovered between the two trying to think of a way of opening a conversation with Dr Strang, but while she hesitated Anna Wakefield called to him from the chaise longue she was relaxing upon.

'Give me a cigarette, Paul darling!'

He obeyed, and then she swung her legs over the side to make room for him to sit down. 'I can't stay long,' he said.

'Why ever not?' Anna pouted. 'We hardly ever see you at all. You come once in an age and then you grudge every minute you spend away from the natives!'

He smiled a little condescendingly. 'I do come to the island on business, after all, and sick people are my business. Since the islanders are in the majority here and also are less well-fed and less able to take care of themselves than the rest, it seems reasonable that I should devote more time to them.'

'Oh, you!' She looked at him with a mixture of despair and affection and then turned to Helen. 'What can I do with him, Miss Davis?'

Helen was slightly embarrassed by the possessiveness the other woman displayed towards Paul Strang but, still hoping to have an opportunity of sowing a few seeds of propaganda, she said, 'Well, he is right, isn't he? But Dr Strang can't possibly do all that needs doing on his short visits. I know I haven't been here long myself, but I can see ways of improving the service we provide–'

'Oh, please don't start talking shop, you people,' their hostess pleaded. 'I want a drink, so be an angel, Paul.'

He got up. 'Can I get you something, Miss Davis?' She refused and he looked at Colin. 'Fraser appears to be asleep.'

When he returned from the trolley, Helen put on her most professional voice and said, 'I hope I will be able to discuss the hospital with you before you leave the island, Doctor. There are several things I'm not satisfied with.'

'I don't doubt it,' he replied. 'There are many things I'm extremely dissatisfied with, but whether anything can be done about them is another question. Of course one can make excuses for the present state of affairs–'

Feeling that Colin was being attacked when he was unable to defend himself, Helen leapt into the breach. 'There is a good reason, not an excuse, for one part of it. It's months since the last nurse left so suddenly–'

'Suddenly is right,' put in Anna Wakefield, a malicious smile on her lovely face as she stared into her glass. 'Poor Georgina!'

Hastily Paul Strang said, 'Stop talking nonsense, Anna!' and then told Helen, 'We'll talk things over tomorrow morning. I don't have to leave too early. I must go now and–' he threw a scornful glance at Colin who was still asleep, 'I think I'd better take you and Fraser home.'

Helen closed the door of the McFarlanes' bungalow behind her and leaned against it.

She was tired but reluctant to go to bed. Sleep would not come easily to her that night. Her mind was too troubled to let her rest. Over and over again she asked herself questions she could not begin to answer; questions about Colin, about Anna Wakefield, about Paul Strang, and most disturbing of all, questions about Georgina Grey. There was a mystery connected with the nurse who had worked with Colin before Helen came to Victoria and everyone seemed to know the explanation except Helen. Meg McFarlane had clearly been concealing something when the other nurse was mentioned on Helen's first day in Victoria though it had not struck Helen forcibly at the time. Now, recalling the expression on Anna Wakefield's face as she said, 'Suddenly is right', Helen was convinced there was something she must know about.

Slow, quiet footsteps breaking the silence of the house startled her and she sighed with relief when she saw Meg coming through the rear hall door with a tray in her hand.

'So there you are, ma dear,' the older woman said in surprise. 'I heard you come in and went to make you a warm drink, but when I took it to your room you were not there. Are you all right?'

Helen pushed back her hair with a weary gesture. 'Yes. I'm all right,' but her voice was so shaky that Meg was concerned.

She put the tray down on a table and came to the young nurse. 'Come away to your bed this second, dearie,' she said gently, and within a few minutes Helen was sitting in bed, her hands cupped around a glass of hot milk and Meg perched beside her.

'Now, I hope you won't think I'm being a busybody, Helen,' she began cautiously, 'I don't mean to fuss, but I told you when you came that I might try to look after you more than you want—'

Helen put a hand on her arm. 'I don't mind if you do fuss a bit. You're kind and—' her voice began to tremble again, 'I – oh, dear– What's the matter with me?'

Taking the glass away, Meg put her arms round the weeping girl. 'There now, there now, it's all right,' she crooned soothingly. 'You're tired and homesick. That's perfectly understandable, isn't it? The way you've worked since you came here, and then you miss your family and friends. It's a long time ago, but I well remember how I felt when I first left Scotland. It was as if invisible cords were trying to draw me back there – and it was not as bad for me, having Angus at ma side. You have no-one of your own near to comfort you when things get a little trying–' she held Helen away from her so that she could look into her face, 'and they are just now, are they not – a little trying?'

Helen nodded. 'A little.'

'This can't go on, you know. You must take things more easily. You're attempting to put right the neglect of months all in a couple of weeks and it's too much.'

'It isn't really the work,' Helen said in a thin voice, and noticed that Meg stiffened slightly. 'There's something else bothering me.'

'To do with Colin Fraser?'

'No, not Colin. It's–' Helen hesitated, wondering how to say what she wanted to say, and then blurted out, 'Nurse Grey! Why did she leave?'

It was out, and it seemed to Helen that the question had not come as a surprise to Meg, rather that it had been expected. 'Georgina?'

'Yes. There's some mystery about her and it makes me feel uncomfortable. You can tell me what happened, can't you?'

'It's all over now, dear, and in my opinion best forgotten,' the Scotswoman said firmly, as she might have spoken to the children in her school. But Helen was not a child.

'You may be right, but until I know what this is about, how can I forget it?'

'I suppose you ought to be told since you have somehow guessed that you were being kept in the dark. I had hoped you need not know.' Meg paused, looking down at her hands clenched in her lap, and then went on slowly, 'It was very sad. Such a pretty girl, with the loveliest auburn hair. Long, it was; well past her shoulders when she wore it loose. That's how it was when – when they found her.'

Helen stared. 'You talk as if – as if–'

'Spread out like a bright cape it was–'

'What happened?'

'Oh, my dear, don't let it upset you too much. It's over now.'

'What happened?'

'It was an accident. A tragic accident. Poor Gina fell from the cliff behind the hospital. Poor wee lass!'

At seven o'clock the next morning, Helen was dressed for work and standing by her bedroom window. This was wide-open and the air was cool and fresh. She hoped it would sweep the dullness from her brain and perhaps the pallor from her cheeks. Just when she needed to be at her best, to make

111

a good impression on Paul Strang and convince him she knew what she was talking about, she felt and looked thoroughly washed-out. She had slept so badly. All night long she had tossed and turned trying to wipe out the picture that dominated her mind – the picture of a young girl's broken body at the foot of a cliff; a girl with auburn hair spread out around her like a cape.

Poor Georgina!

Meg said she fell – from the cliff behind the hospital. Her words had drummed in Helen's brain through the weary hours – the loveliest auburn hair – past her shoulders – that's how it was when they found her – and questions had followed, clamouring for attention. Frightening questions.

If Georgina fell when she was near the hospital, wouldn't she be in uniform? And wouldn't her hair be pinned up? If her hair was loose and she was not on duty, how did she come to fall from that spot? Did she go up to the highest accessible point on the island for some other reason than that the hospital was there?

Did she go up there – that pretty, auburn-haired girl – deliberately to throw herself to her death?

Chapter Nine

At seven-thirty, Helen heard a car drive up to the front gate. Good. Colin had arrived early to collect her on this important morning, to her relief and surprise considering the state he had been in when she and Paul Strang left him at his bungalow the night before. It was too bad of him to drink too much when so many things depended on changing Dr Strang's opinion of him. They must convince the Medical Officer that Colin was capable of running a hospital in all its departments, including surgery, but that before this could be done efficiently he must be given the necessary medical supplies and funds.

She took a quick glance in the mirror. She was still pale but thought she looked reasonably alert and composed. Somehow she knew that she would need to keep up at least the appearance of self-possession for Colin's sake. Otherwise he might go to pieces. He needed her to give him confidence. Funny how a person can seem to have loads of assurance, yet be so unsure of themselves.

Picking up her case, she went quickly through the house and out on to the verandah. It was with a strange mixture of emotions that she saw, not Colin's battered red sports model, but a sleek, white saloon, at the gate, and that the man talking to Meg on the path was Paul Strang.

She went slowly towards them, striving to appear unflurried. 'Good morning, Dr Strang,' she said.

He returned her greeting, adding, 'I hope I'm not too early.'

'Och, Helen's always ready by this, though–' Meg broke off, seeing the plea in Helen's eyes, and forbore to comment on Colin's habit of arriving much later to pick her up. 'Never mind now.'

'I'll drive you to the hospital then, nurse,' Dr Strang said. 'I haven't a lot of time and you said you wanted to talk to me.'

Meg walked with them to the car, telling Helen that there was extra food in her lunch basket as she had eaten no breakfast.

The car was a powerful American one which Helen remembered seeing at the Wakefields'. It made easy work of the rough, steep road up to the hospital. There, as they went into the building, she resolutely averted her eyes from the cliff edge.

She would not think about Georgina today.

Thomas hurried to meet them, immaculate in white cotton pants and shirt. Helen guessed that this early visit of the M.O. was not entirely unexpected, for though her assistant was always clean and bright-eyed, the ward and the patients were spruced up unusually early. As they stood at one end of the ward looking around, the door at the far end opened and the two cured lepers hobbled in carrying large bunches of brilliantly-coloured flowers which they stuffed inartistically into a varied assortment of jars and tins around the room. Then one of them came to Helen and presented her shyly with a posy of hibiscus.

'Thank you so much, Tere, and you Kio,' she said warmly, and then to the doctor, 'These are our gardeners.' The two ex-patients beamed with pride and than limped away.

Paul Strang said, 'I thought the grounds were looking remarkably tidy when I was here yesterday. This is the explanation, is it?'

Helen looked at him uncertainly. His dark face was serious and his voice so noncommittal that she could not be sure whether he was criticizing her or not. Being on edge, she inclined to believe he was, and replied defensively, 'The men are not ill. There's nothing more we can do for them medically and since their families won't have them back they must stay here. I don't see why they shouldn't do a useful job if they are fit enough. It's good for their self-respect.'

He looked at her in silence for a moment and then said quietly, 'I agree.' A fleeting smile softened his features as he watched her face. Indignation dissolved and surprise was replaced by slight embarrassment. 'I'm glad to find that your mind is not so narrow – professionally – that you lose interest in a person when his medical treatment is finished. That is important here, where we have no vast welfare service to take over when our job is done. I congratulate you on the way you've got to grips with this problem, and so quickly too.'

'Thank you, Doctor, but I can't take too much credit,' she admitted. 'The men are not exactly eager workers; I have to keep an eye on them or they lie down under the trees and go to sleep.'

'But that's an indigenous characteristic of

the Pacific Islander, nurse. You really must temper your crusading zeal to local conditions.'

Again Helen felt a little irritated. This man had a way of saying the wrong thing; of rubbing her up the wrong way. Now his remark about 'crusading zeal' made her feel like a pushing 'do-gooder'. 'I will try,' she said, biting back her annoyance.

They went to see the two malaria cases who were sitting up in their beds waiting for their relatives to bring in their breakfast bowls after cooking the food in the outside kitchen hut. The patients were almost ready for discharge now and were becoming increasingly difficult about staying in bed; they protested to Dr Strang in voluble Polynesian and he answered fluently. Then he said to Helen, 'I've told them as soon as they are fit enough to get up Missy Nurse will give them so much work to do they'll wish they were back in bed.'

In the office, Helen found a tumbler for her flowers and put them on the table. Paul Strang leaned against the wall and said, 'This is all very different from what you've been used to, I'm sure, nurse. Do you think you will cope?'

She was standing at the wash-basin. Now

she turned the tap off and said slowly, 'It is different, of course. I expected that. As to whether I will cope – how can I tell yet?' She looked up and spoke to his reflection in the small mirror on the wall. 'Have I made such a poor start?'

'Not at all, nurse,' he replied with infuriating patience, 'I've told you already how impressed I am with the change you've brought about in the short time you've been here, but there are so many aspects to this thing. Please don't misunderstand me–'

She swung round and gripped the edge of the washbasin behind her. 'I don't think I misunderstand you, Doctor Strang,' she said quietly and steadily. 'You consider me unsuitable for this post. You've made that perfectly clear. You were generous enough to say I'd made a big change here, but obviously you don't think a capacity for hard work is all that important; not when set against my failings!'

He had not moved a muscle while she was talking. When she stopped and turned her back on him, washing her hands energetically he took a step or two towards her. 'Nurse Davis, there really is no need for you to upset yourself like this. I merely wonder if such a young girl can withstand the pressures encountered in a position such as you find yourself in. And, as I said, the physical strain is only part of it.'

She picked up a nail-brush and rubbed soap carefully on to the bristles. 'I am twenty-three, Doctor,' she told him, still managing to keep her voice calm though she was feeling far from that, 'I have been nursing for five years and am fully-qualified. I am in perfect health. As to my character – perhaps you would like to see copies of my references. The Medical Commission were apparently satisfied that I was fitted for the post.' She rinsed her hands and pulled out the plug. When the gurgling of the water had died away, she reached for the towel but it was not on its rail. Paul Strang was holding it ready for her. She took it with a brief 'Thanks' and then went on, 'If you have reason to think otherwise please say so bluntly.'

Catching a glimpse of herself in the mirror as she replaced the towel on the rail – her cheeks were flushed and her eyes their deepest blue, sparkling with anger – she told herself this was wrong; this was not the way to convince him she was efficient and self-possessed and all the other things she wanted him to believe about her. She was more likely to confirm his poor opinion of her. And that would do no-one any good. Not herself, not Colin, and certainly not the Islanders. Yet she could not stop. All her weariness and anxiety seemed to well up inside her and demand release somehow.

'You put me in a difficult position,' the doctor said, and she snapped back, 'Then perhaps I can make it easier for you. Your disapproval of me is connected with Dr Fraser, isn't it? When you came to Victoria yesterday I was spending my day off with him, and because you dislike Colin you took a dim view. So now you conclude that I am unsuitable for the job.'

He pushed his fingers through his black hair and then took a leisurely walk round the table. Eventually, perching on a corner of it, he said, 'I was going to say that my opinion of Dr Fraser has nothing to do with my misgivings as to your appointment here, but that would not be true. There is a link and, though I would rather not discuss it, it is probably better for all concerned to have the record straight from the outset.' He felt in the pocket of his light bush jacket and brought out a pipe. 'Would you mind if I smoke?' She shook her head and he lit the pipe. When it was drawing satisfactorily he looked thoughtfully at her and said, 'This goes deeper than any petty personal grievance, Nurse Davis. You may find this difficult to understand, but it goes right to the basic indispensable requirement in any activity which causes whites to be in the position of instructors or guides to coloured people. If they don't trust us we can do nothing. A teacher must set a good example or how can he expect the pupil to learn better ways? You see the sense in that?'

'Of course I do,' she said evenly, and waited for him to go on.

'Well–' he continued, 'human nature being what it is, a bad influence has more immediate appeal than a good one, and years of slogging labour can be undone in weeks. So that a couple like the McFarlanes work for decades building up confidence and raising standards – moral and material – only to see their efforts undermined in a fraction of the time.' He paused, drawing deeply on the pipe clenched between his teeth, and again Helen waited. But the seconds dragged past and he said nothing.

When she could stand the heavy silence no longer she said: 'You are saying that Colin Fraser is setting a bad example–'

'Can you say he is setting a good one?' he

countered swiftly.

'No!' she blazed. 'I don't pretend he is! And I can tell you why he isn't, though you may find this difficult to understand.' She stressed the 'you' and the 'this' as she threw his own phrases back at him. 'A "holier than thou" attitude does not usually go with an ability to see the other person's point of view, but I'll try. You talk about building up confidence in the islanders. What about the confidence of your own colleague? Why do you treat Dr Fraser worse than you would a first-year medical student? Why do you refuse to let him practise as a qualified man has the right to do? Since you know so much about the subject, you must know that if you make it obvious you have no confidence in a man, he will very soon lose confidence in himself. And when that happens–' she paused to take a deep breath and continued more quietly, 'if he drinks a little too much – who is to blame?'

He prodded the tobacco in the bowl of his pipe carefully before replying. 'The doctor has a persuasive advocate in you, nurse; you present his case very well and he should consider himself fortunate. But nevertheless I must plead not guilty to the charge you have laid against me. I hardly feel inclined to take responsibility for his drinking habits.' He met her glance. 'If I treat the man as incompetent it is simply because experience has proved him to be so, and–'

'How can you say that?' she demanded angrily. 'What chance has he had to prove anything? Look at this place!' She waved her arm to take in the whole hospital. 'No decent stock of medicines, practically no instruments! No provision for surgery at all! How can anyone work under such conditions? It's very unfair to judge when things are so inadequate. It's like – like condemning a horse for being slow when his legs are tied together!'

He stood up and went across to the window. He looked out for a moment and then, his back still towards her, said with a coolness that made her own manner, she realized, appear to be almost hysterical. 'Fifty years ago a man came to this island. He had retired from medical practice and was taking a long sea-voyage before settling down to a quiet life in Bournemouth. The ship was here three weeks for repairs and in that time the doctor got to know some of the local people. When they learned his profession they flocked to him for help and he did not turn them away. The ship sailed

– without him. He never left Victoria. He died here twenty years later at the age of eighty and in those years his surgery was never more than a hut of hibiscus branches and palm leaves and his equipment the few instruments he was carrying with him as souvenirs of his work, supplemented occasionally by odd things he could beg from friends back home. He tackled everything – from childbirth to toothache and broken bones to blood-poisoning – and had the complete trust and affection of the people.'

Helen glared at his back. How could she reply to this story? She could not let him think he had demolished her with his pompous tale. 'That's all very well,' she began, and then bit her lip. That sounded childish. Oh, now she was forgetting what she meant to say. What was it? Ah.– 'Just because one man struggled against great odds and made a success is no reason to refuse another man a better chance. If it were there'd be no progress. Doctors managed without anaesthetics and X-rays years ago because they had to, but they take full advantage of these discoveries now.'

'True, but it doesn't really affect my argument, nurse.' He turned to face her. 'I'm sorry we should have this disagreement.

Perhaps a little longer here will show you your mistake. Now–' he looked at his watch, 'I must go. I borrowed Mrs Wakefield's car and she wants it back.'

'But you can't – I mean, I must talk to you,' Helen objected.

He smiled slightly. 'You already have, nurse, and I don't think it would serve any useful purpose to prolong the discussion. We must agree to differ for the moment and, as I said, time may alter your views.'

'Or yours,' she put in quickly.

His smile broadened but he did not answer. He went to the door and in desperation Helen called him back.

'Doctor, I'm sorry if I'm keeping Mrs Wakefield waiting for her car, but I must make one point. We've been talking about various people but the most important ones have been left out. The patients. What about them? Is it fair to them to deprive them of the best medical care possible just because of personal feelings about Dr Fraser and myself?'

'If I did that it would not only be unfair, it would be completely against the ethics of my profession,' he replied seriously. 'In fact, the islanders are not suffering any neglect under present conditions. If I thought they were I would not tolerate those conditions for another minute. As it is, with the arrangements existing for getting in contact with me or my assistant, I can turn a blind eye. You will no doubt learn the reasons for this unsatisfactory compromise in due course. I had hoped for an improvement when I heard the post of nurse here was filled– Please don't interrupt! I'm in a hurry, and you asked me to be frank – I hoped an older woman would be appointed after what happened–'

Suddenly, the door was thrown back and Colin Fraser burst in. 'Well, here you are, gossiping like two old women!'

Helen wondered anxiously if he had overheard Paul Strang's remarks. He could have been near the unlatched door for some time without them knowing. If he had, better part them as quickly as possible. 'Dr Strang drove me up,' she told Colin nervously. 'He has to go now.'

He smiled at her, but his eyes were hard. 'Don't let me break up an interesting conversation.' He turned to Paul Strang. 'You were saying–?'

Strang studied the other doctor silently. 'You should cut down on that locally-distilled hooch, Fraser,' he said eventually in an icy voice. He went to the door, paused to say, 'I'll be back in a month's time. I don't think I can manage it sooner,' and then stalked out.

Chapter Ten

'Damned bloody prig!' Colin spat out furiously, clenching his hands. 'Sorry, Helen, but can you wonder that I loathe the sight of him?'

She went to stand in front of him and put her hands on his shoulders. 'I know he can be infuriating–'

'That's putting it mildly!'

'Colin, dear, listen to me. He was right – about you drinking too much. Oh, yes he was. You know it, too. So please, for my sake as well as your own, but most of all for the sake of the patients, you will try to cut it down at least, won't you? Please?'

He looked at her earnest young face and swiftly his anger melted away. He put his arms round her gently and held her close. 'Oh, Helen, my sweet girl,' he murmured huskily, 'I will try. I can do it, too, with you beside me. A man can do anything if he has someone to do it for; someone to be strong for. When I started this heavy drinking I was so miserable – lonely – with no-one to give a damn whether I lived or died – nothing seemed to matter any more. Then you came,' he smoothed back her hair and kissed her forehead lingeringly, 'and from the moment I saw you, so young and – untouched, somehow, so lovely in that simple dress you were wearing, your hair shining and soft, I began to come back to life. And when you looked at me with those glorious, clear blue eyes, I felt hope rising in me. Darling, I need you so much. If I lose you–'

'Sh – Colin,' she whispered, and clasped her hands behind his neck bringing his head down so that she could reach to kiss his lips, 'You're not going to lose me. I don't get lost that easily. So long as you need me I'll be there, I promise.'

They clung to each other tightly for a long moment. Then Helen drew away, holding on to his hands. 'This won't do, Doctor,' she said with a tremulous smile, 'we have work to do.'

'Not just now, darling,' he coaxed, but she stood firm.

'Now this minute, Doctor, and from now on my name is Nurse Davis when we're on duty.'

'Slave-driver!'

'Exactly,' she agreed cheerfully, 'but I will

give you a nice cup of coffee while we make plans.' As she unpacked milk, sugar and coffee from the lunch-basket and made the drinks – boiling milk on the small oil-heater that also served to boil water for sterilizing instruments – Helen began to talk about the ideas that had been forming in her head as she worked at the hospital. 'I'm sure there ought to be somewhere nearer the villages where people could come for advice, or mothers could bring their babies – or come for pre-natal care – things like that. Can you think of a suitable place? If not we could build one.'

Colin grinned. 'You weren't joking when you said we had work to do, were you? Don't forget there's only two of us. We can't be in half a dozen places at once.'

'I know, but I have another idea–'

'I'll bet you have!'

'Listen! Oh – you can get the cups out, please – what was I saying? Oh, yes. You see, the clinic will give us the chance of getting to know the people and perhaps spotting those who need hospital treatment but would not volunteer to be in-patients of their own accord. When they get to know us and lose their suspicion they won't be afraid.'

'Great!' he remarked drily. 'So we have a

full hospital up here and a clinic bursting its sides in the village. Then the white community and the school and–'

'Pick them up a minute.'

'Eh? Oh, the cups.'

He picked them up while Helen spread a white cloth over part of the table and then set them out again. They sat down and spent a contented half-hour discussing ways and means of providing a good, efficient service for the islanders. Helen made notes as they talked and her enthusiasm infected Colin so that instead of trying to curb her eagerness he became as keen as she was.

And as they schemed and planned, a shadow hovered over them. The shadow of a man they never mentioned but who dominated their thoughts. The shadow of Paul Strang.

The school run by Mrs McFarlane was made of corrugated iron and was furnished with rough wooden benches and a few tables. It did not matter, though, that it lacked many refinements in the way of decoration and equipment. When Helen walked towards the school next morning she was greeted by such a joyful sound of children singing with all their heart and soul that she realized that here at least material poverty was a matter of minor importance when compared with the wealth of spiritual resources these youngsters possessed. She stood at the open door until the chorus finished and then went inside.

Meg McFarlane was at one end of the single large room the building consisted of, with a blackboard at her side. Seeing Helen she waved happily. 'So you found your way, dear. Good. Come along and meet the class. Children, here is Nurse Davis come to see you. What do you say?'

Helen laughed at the volume of noise the twenty-odd voices managed to produce as they cried, 'Welcome, nurse, Welcome!'

She thanked them and Meg said, 'I did think of trying to get them to say "Boro da" or "Cymru am byth" but it seemed a little unfair to them when they are struggling with English to confuse them with Welsh words. I've been telling them a little about your homeland.' She pointed to the map of Wales on the blackboard. 'Now would you like to look at the drawings they did of it?'

They walked round looking at the pictures pinned up on the walls, and then Meg said, 'I'll take the young ones outside for nature study so that you can have your chat with the older ones.'

About half-a-dozen boys and as many girls remained after Meg had left with her section. Helen stood facing them, feeling rather shy. This was a new experience for her. 'Boys and girls,' she began, 'I want to talk to you about my work as a nurse. You all know that a nurse is a person who helps other people when they are ill.' She spoke slowly and distinctly, watching the faces of her audience for signs of incomprehension, as she told of the duties of a nurse in the simplest language she could.

The young people, aged between thirteen and sixteen, listened with apparent interest and understanding, and when she came to the end of her talk a buzz of chatter broke out.

'I have something else to say to you all,' she said, and the noise died away. 'I want you to think about what I have told you and tell your fathers and mothers of it. Then, if any of you feel you would like to learn more, I will come again.'

When Helen came away from the school, waved off by all the children, Colin was waiting for her in the car.

She got in beside him and he said, 'You look happy, darling.'

She nodded. 'What a wonderful spirit

there is in that little school, Colin,' she said. 'If we can get that in our hospital and clinic, it won't matter if things are a bit makeshift and shabby. And I think there's a very good chance of some really useful student nurses coming forward.'

'Don't expect too much,' he warned. 'They are always full of curiosity about anything new, and they would be interested in you as well.'

'Perhaps, but we will find out who really wants to learn about nursing when I start giving regular lessons. Then the best of them – when they leave school – can come and help at the hospital and the clinic.'

'Oh, yes, I'm supposed to be taking you to see a possible building for this clinic of yours–' 'Ours,' she put in. '–of ours,' he amended. He started the car and drove off along the dusty road. On either side, huts were dotted haphazardly among vegetable patches and groups of palm and fruit trees and, being mid-afternoon, the shady areas beneath the trees sheltered many a slumbering islander. '"Mad dogs and Englishmen",' commented Colin. 'Noel Coward didn't mention Welsh girls.'

He drove on, and the huts became more numerous, closer together; the scattered refuse more unsightly. 'I did tell you the place I had in mind was not in the most salubrious part of the island, didn't I?'

'It would be no use if it was,' she replied. 'The clinic must be where the people are.'

'So long as you're prepared,' he said. 'You know,' he went on after a moment, 'this idea of yours for training some of the kids as nurses is going to take up a lot of time.'

'Yes, I do know that. But I'm sure it's worthwhile, not only because we need assistance. As well as that, the scheme will provide useful and interesting jobs for a few of the better-educated children.'

'Oh, it's fine in theory—'

'And it will be fine in practice, you'll see. We'll fit our lectures in as best we can—'

'Our lectures?'

'Of course, didn't I tell you?' she asked innocently. 'While I'm doing baby care, hygiene, nutrition, etc. you will be dealing with anatomy and physiology.'

He sighed deeply. 'And I thought when I first met you that you were fragile. Wouldn't have much stamina. Ha! You have the constitution of an ox combined with a will of iron!'

'Thank you for those kind words, sir,' she laughed. 'Oh, are we there?'

The road had become gradually rougher as they drove and now Colin pulled over on to a clearing in the middle of which stood a fairly large building made of concrete slabs. The windows were broken but otherwise there was little that could be damaged. Helen took a good look at it and then nodded. 'It has possibilities,' she decided.

About three weeks later, Helen was having a rare afternoon of leisure. She was stretched in a long chair on the McFarlanes' verandah writing to Mair Phillips and Jonah the cat was enjoying the sunshine with her. The letter was overdue, but until recently things had been so unsettled that she was afraid of betraying her troubled state of mind to her friend. Since everything had begun to go well, she just had not had time to write.

Angus McFarlane came up the path and took the verandah steps in one bound. 'Hello, there,' he called. 'You must have broken a leg to be sitting down. Oh, you're writing I see. I'll not disturb you.'

'It can wait,' she smiled, putting it aside.

'Just for a minute then. C'mon, Jonah, move yourself.' He lifted the reluctant animal from its chair and seated himself. 'I've scarcely had a word with you since you arrived, Helen.'

'There was quite a lot to do.'

'I know fine, and you've tackled it all with zest.'

'Dr Fraser and I,' she said meaningfully, 'have great plans for the island.'

He nodded and stroked his reddish beard thoughtfully. 'Yes – Fraser. I don't want to sound like an old washer-woman, but I must say that young man has pulled himself together remarkably in the last few weeks. I've noticed a big change.'

'I'm afraid he had got rather discouraged, but that's all over now.'

The clergyman looked uncomfortable. 'Well – er – let's hope so, I'm sure.'

Helen bit her lip. 'I'm not such a Doubting Thomas, thank goodness,' she said sternly.

'Sorry, my dear. I just hope you won't be disappointed.'

'I know. But I think sometimes a little more faith and charity would bring better results than simply hoping.'

He bowed his grizzled head. 'You are really belabouring me with the Good Book, aren't you?' he asked ruefully. 'You have a point there, though. I believe that to expect the best of a person is often to obtain the best.'

'Well then–'

He held up a warning hand. 'I also believe in tempering confidence with caution, especially in certain cases. You see, my dear, we have known Colin Fraser much longer than you have. That is why we have doubts. Nothing would delight us more than to have those doubts proved unnecessary. Believe me.'

'I do believe you,' she said, reaching forward to put her hand in his. 'I haven't known Colin long, but perhaps I understand him better than anyone else.'

She did not notice the look of sadness in his eyes as he got up, and she did not see him shake his head, because at that moment Meg McFarlane came running up the path to them and panted, 'Helen, you're here! There's a wee bairn – very ill. Will you come?'

Helen was on her feet already. 'Where? Tell me as much as you can.'

'In one of the huts near the school. One of my senior girls told me. I went to see. The baby was shivering, but sweating too, and it had a dry cough.'

Helen said fearfully: 'It sounds like pneumonia,' and turned to Angus. 'Can you take me?' He nodded and loped off.

Meg asked if she could help. 'We'll need blankets and hot water bottles,' Helen told her, adding, 'we'll have to get Colin. He said he'd be doing his reports this afternoon.'

'Angus will take you to the Doctor's bungalow on the way. I'll get these things and then I must get back to the school. Tell Angus it's Pila's baby – she used to be our housemaid – they called their wee son Andrew as a compliment to him.'

Mrs McFarlane went inside and Helen followed to pick up her small case. When she came out again the pony cart was at the front gate and she climbed hurriedly aboard.

Soon they were rattling away from the scattered pleasant houses of the white community and towards the densely-populated native villages. About half-way between these two extremes, Angus stopped the cart outside an isolated bungalow standing in an untidy garden. 'This is Fraser's place,' he said, and without a word Helen jumped down and ran to the front door. She pushed it back. 'Colin!'

There was no reply and she called again, walking into the dark hall. Still no response, and she went to one of the doors leading off the hall. It opened on to a lounge. No-one there. She heard a sound behind her and swung round. 'Colin?'

But it was Angus. 'He's no' here,' he said bluntly.

'He said– He might be resting.'

Angus crossed to another door at the back of the hall and banged on it. Then he flung it open. 'No,' he called. 'This is his bed-room, and he's no' here.'

'Let's get to the baby, then,' Helen called back. She picked up Colin's medical bag from a chair and ran out into the sun.

Close on her heels, McFarlane said, 'I have an idea where he might be.' The words came reluctantly, but Helen didn't notice.

She asked eagerly: 'Is it far?'

'No, and it's in the right direction.'

'We'll try it then.'

Another few minutes jolting ride and they were stopping outside a native hut, one of a group within a circle of jacaranda trees. 'You wait here, Helen,' Angus said. 'I'll go in.'

'No. I'll go in while you turn the cart round ready for a quick move.' Helen ran to the hut and called, 'Colin! Are there?'

Two or three curious children gathered to stare. She called again, and the drape over the door-space was pushed aside.

Colin stood there, blinking in the strong sunlight, and obviously very drunk. And

141

beyond him, in the shadows, was a lovely island girl. A girl Helen had seen before – on the jetty when she and Colin returned from the atoll!

Chapter Eleven

Helen stared for a moment of bewildered disgust at the half-ashamed, half-defiant young doctor. He was wearing only a pair of creased trousers, and pushed back his over-long unkempt hair as he returned her look. 'Colin, you must come. Quickly!' she told him urgently.

'Come where?' His voice was thick and indistinct, and she was torn by indecision. Should she leave him and get to the child as soon as possible? Even if she spared valuable minutes getting him to realize the seriousness of the situation, would he be of any use in his present state?

She went closer to him. 'Please, Doctor. 'There's a child desperately ill; I think it's pneumonia. Come with us now!'

Angus McFarlane had come to join the group. 'You'd best leave him,' he advised contemptuously, but something made Helen try again.

It was a feeling that this was crucial; that a turning point had been reached and the way the next few moments worked out would be the making or breaking of Colin as a doctor and as a man. Now, though the vision of a child lying in some unhygienic hut fighting for breath was vividly before her, she was not solely concerned with the young patient. 'Please, Colin–' she begged.

He looked past her at Angus, his eyes clearer but very angry.

'She'd best leave him, had she?' he demanded with quiet fury. 'You think I'm useless, don't you? Well, we'll see!' He turned to the island girl who hovered in the doorway of the hut, an uncertain smile on her beautiful face. 'My shirt!' he rapped out.

She disappeared at once and came back with the garment which she helped him into. Her hands caressed his neck as she put the collar straight, and she whispered, 'You leave Janita? No, you not go.' Her arms tightened and her slim brown body pressed against him.

Helen ran to the trap and clambered blindly in, followed by Angus who flicked the pony with the reins. As Robbie began to canter away, Colin leapt on to the step and pulled himself aboard the now fast-moving cart. He spotted his medical bag beside Helen's feet and said, 'You went to my place?

I – I meant to stay in–'

'It doesn't matter,' she said coolly.

Angus stopped the pony at a hut near the schoolhouse and got down to help Helen alight. They hurried up a path neatly lined with white-washed rocks of coral and into the hut. A boy of about two years was lying on a low, roughly-made bed in one corner with a piece of bright cotton material for covering. A young woman was kneeling at his side and a dozen or so anxious-looking spectators were standing around with doleful expressions.

The young woman glanced up and, when she saw Angus, began to moan. He stooped to speak to her.

'Don't be afraid, Pila. I'm not here because your son is dying. I've brought the Doctor and nurse to get him well. Now I am going outside, and all these other folk must go too. The boy needs air.'

Helen smiled her gratitude as he firmly ushered out all the reluctant relatives except the mother, father and grandmother. Colin was on his knees beside the gasping, sweating boy taking his temperature. It was 105°. 'It's pneumonia all right,' he said.

As Helen covered the small patient with blankets, she noticed a change in the sound of his laboured breathing. The child was literally fighting for his life. She met Colin's eyes. He had noticed too, and his face was set.

He said grimly: 'He has an obstruction in the trachea.'

This was what Helen had been afraid of. With the wind-pipe blocked, the little patient might die within minutes unless prompt and skilful action were taken. And was Colin Fraser, out of touch and practice, far from sober, lacking in faith in himself – was he capable of taking the necessary measure?

She had defended him against his critics and believed herself in the right. But now she was frightened. A child's life hung in the balance. Whether this brown-skinned little boy – Andrew – lived to play in the sun again depended on Colin.

Helen prayed to herself fervently, and found herself wishing Paul Strang were there. However arrogant and brusque the other doctor might be, she was certain he would be cool and efficient in any emergency. He was many miles away, though.

She looked beyond Colin and found the dark, imploring eyes of young Andrew's mother fixed upon her. Then Colin was turning to her. 'Helen–' It was almost a groan.

She reached across the bed to put her hand briefly on his, as if she could somehow infuse strength into him. Making a great effort to keep her voice steady, she said, 'What do you want me to do, Doctor?'

'Is there any boiling water?' he asked. Pila nodded vigorously. 'Good.' Reaching into his bag, he produced a piece of thin rubber tubing and a narrow-bladed knife. Handing these to Helen to be sterilized, he said quietly, 'There ought to be a proper tracheotomy set here, but there isn't, so I'll have to improvise for the time being. It won't be the first time rubber tubing has been used as a cannula.'

While Helen was busy, he tried to persuade the relatives to go outside, but they refused and he enlisted their aid in holding the boy still. Andrew was semi-conscious now and oblivious to what was happening.

A folded blanket was placed under his shoulders and his head held back. Colin cleaned the little throat and picked up the knife from the dish Helen held. The atmosphere was oppressive; the only sound that of the boy's strained breathing and a subdued murmuring from the waiting crowd outside.

Doctor and nurse knelt on either side of the bed. The knife was raised and plunged swiftly with an upward movement to pierce the trachea, withdrawn and dropped on to the dish; then the piece of tubing was inserted.

As the incision was made, a horrified gasp had issued from the watching parents, but they had controlled themselves immediately and when it was over and they could see the dramatic change in the child they were equally restrained in their joy.

As he and Helen strapped the tube into place, Colin said, 'This seems to have eased the respiration considerably, but I must have the proper instruments and some more penicillin as soon as possible. I'll give him an injection now, then leave you in charge while I go to the radio station.' He stood up. 'With any luck we should get the supplies before nightfall.'

Helen heard the clamour as the crowd of waiting relatives and neighbours gathered around the departing doctor, eager for news. Then the rattling as the pony-trap trotted away. A good thing Angus had waited. Hope there is no hitch in getting the things flown in. Suppose the plane was out of action or otherwise engaged? So many things could go wrong. Well, this ought to support her argument with Paul Strang if anything would. Here was practical proof that Victoria Island should be better equipped to deal with such emergencies.

She put her fingers on the sleeping boy's wrist. The pulse was much less rapid and shallow, and the temperature – yes, it was down. 100° now. The child was still ill, but with his respiratory difficulty eased the drugs would be able to take their effect. Andrew would get well. She closed her eyes for a second as she thanked God for this recovery. For two recoveries, she thought.

Colin had risen to the occasion in an almost miraculous way. When the moment for action came, his hand was steady and his eyes clear and straight.

When school was over for the day, Meg called at the hut to see if there was anything she could do to help. Later she confessed to Helen that she was very surprised to find the patient still alive and the young nurse was delighted to give Colin all the credit possible and to omit to mention where she and Angus had found him and in what condition.

The Scotswoman said, 'The entire family is outside and they are seething with excitement and curiosity over what's been going on. So am I, if I'm to be honest. The wee laddie looks a lot better than when I saw him last.'

Helen explained about the emergency tracheotomy Colin had had to carry out to enable the boy to breathe, and the older woman looked impressed.

'It seems he can do it when he wants to,' she commented.

Colin returned at this and, after checking on the patient, told Helen that the message had been sent and that the plane would be taking off with the necessary supplies immediately.

Meg asked if the child would need watching all night and, when Colin said he would, replied that she would go home then and send along coffee and sandwiches for nurse and doctor. Then she would return to relieve them for a while so they could rest.

In the event, Colin refused to leave, but insisted that Helen go home for some sleep. He came out of the hut with her to have a cigarette before she left.

'I'll be back in two hours and then you can get some sleep,' she told him.

'Don't you dare come back here in less than six hours,' he ordered. 'Everything will be all right now. McFarlane is waiting at the air-strip and will get the things here as quickly as he can. He took my car. Get along now, my dear.'

She hesitated. He looked tired, and older somehow than just a few hours ago. His handsome face was lined and pallid in the fading light as he leaned against a corner-post of the hut. 'Are you sure you won't rest instead of me?' she asked persuasively. 'I think you should. I'm not a bit sleepy.'

'Don't argue, Helen.' He finished his cigarette and ground the stub into the earth with his heel. Then he took her hand and, not looking at her, said, 'Thank you, darling.'

'What for? I didn't do much.'

'You did a great deal, but there's no time to go into that now,' he said huskily, gripping her hand tightly. 'Good-night.'

Helen had a bath and got into bed not expecting to sleep, but after what seemed like only a minute or two she suddenly woke up. What had disturbed her, she wondered. Then as the events of the past hours flooded back into her consciousness, she sat up and looked at her watch. She had been asleep nearly three hours! She got out of bed and slipped her housecoat on. Coming out of her bedroom, she saw through the door leading to the hall, the large figure of a man near the outer door.

It was Angus, and she hurried towards him. 'Is everything all right?' she whispered.

'Oh, aye, everything's fine.'

'The plane arrived with the supplies?'

'Aye, and the wee chap is responding well, so Dr Fraser tells me. He replaced the rubber tube with a silver one while I was there.' Angus smiled. 'So it worked out satisfactorily after all.'

Helen bit her lip and looked thoughtfully at him. 'Angus – I was thinking – I mean–' This was tricky. He was a minister, and she could hardly expect him to–

'Come on, ma dear. Out wi' it,' he encouraged, and she said, 'Well, it's just – does Meg have to know – about Colin being at that place – and that he was – not sober? Must you tell her? He saved the child's life, didn't he?' Without realizing it, she was twisting the belt of her housecoat nervously around her fingers. 'I know you were proved right in what you were saying before all this happened, that it was too soon to think he had changed. But still–'

The clergyman patted her shoulder. 'Still you think he ought to be given yet another chance? No, no–' he held up a hand as she opened her mouth to reply, 'I'm not going to argue, so you needn't quote the parable of forgiving seventy times seven at me. Of course I won't tell my wife or anyone else how or where we found the doctor.'

She sighed with relief. 'Thank you, Angus. Now I must get dressed and take over from him. He must be awfully tired. Did you bring Meg back with you?'

'She wouldna come. Said she'd stand by till you got there.'

'Oh. I'd better hurry then.'

'It won't take us long to get there. I've got Fraser's car – he calls it that, anyway!'

Helen laughed and went to get dressed.

The next thirty-six hours passed with Helen and Colin taking turns to watch the patient, ensuring that the vital air-passage did not become blocked again. The child's parents and grandmother stood quietly by ready to do anything they could, and outside the waiting crowd never seemed to grow any less.

It was late afternoon on the third day

when Colin arrived at the hut in a large car he had borrowed, and explained to Helen that he was going to transfer the child to the hospital where the air was so much cleaner and fresher.

She thought this was a good plan, since it would also allow them to keep an eye on the other patients at the same time. But when he told the boy's mother what he intended doing, he was met with consternation and hostility. Helen watched anxiously, not understanding their words though she realized well enough what was happening. Pila was terrified at the thought of her child being taken to the hospital and appeared to be refusing to consent. Colin was trying to change her mind but finding it impossible. He came to Helen. 'She won't let the boy go to the hospital,' he sighed.

'I gathered that, but why? Does she understand that he will get better more quickly up there?'

He shrugged again, and said she did not believe he would get better at all if she let him go to the hospital, she had the firmly fixed idea that people went there to die.

'Oh, I see,' Helen said, and her shoulders drooped dejectedly.

Noticing this, Colin became defensive.

'What can they expect if they won't let their people come to the hospital until they are in the last stages of illness? It's a vicious circle!'

'I do know what you mean, Colin, but a start has to be made somewhere if things are to improve. Pila is intelligent. She has worked for the McFarlanes, so that she is used to white people and trusts them.'

'Maybe, but that doesn't alter the fact that she is as blindly prejudiced as the most primitive and ignorant woman on the island!' he replied.

'She's frightened. It's her child; her only child.'

'We only want to get him well. Not to steal him from her.'

Helen considered for a moment and then said with some hope, 'I wonder if that's the solution. Perhaps if we let Pila stay with him all the time she would change her mind.'

'I suppose she might,' he agreed, 'and if she did, she could help with the nursing.'

'It's worth trying.'

Colin talked to the distressed mother again while Helen watched with concern, glancing from one to the other. From the doctor using gestures to supplement his imperfect knowledge of the island tongue, to Pila, whose emotions played expressively upon the even features of her olive-skinned face. Fear and determination slowly gave way to thoughtfulness only to return and be overcome again. Finally, the island woman smiled and nodded her assent, and doctor and nurse exchanged a look of thankfulness.

Colin carried the boy out to the car and laid him gently on the back seat. Pila knelt beside him, tucking the blankets around the slight body. These moves had been noted in silence by the ever-present army of relatives, their faces blank, but when Colin and Helen got into the front seat and Colin started the engine, they began to surge forward until they surrounded the car.

With a sigh, the doctor switched off the engine and turned to Pila. She nodded and got out of the car. Her mother was in front of the rest and stood with her arms folded, appearing as likely to be swayed as the sphinx.

While mother and daughter talked, Helen just closed her eyes and waited. That was all she could do in this situation. Either the power of family pressure would prove in-superable or Colin's arguments would conquer it.

Chapter Twelve

Colin said: 'It's like an obstacle race. You get over one problem only to be faced with another.'

Helen smiled weakly. 'I don't think working here will ever be easy going.'

After what seemed like an age, the phalanx began to break up until there was a clear road ahead.

Pila got back into the car and spoke to Colin.

He nodded and said to Helen, 'It's all right so long as grandmother comes too. At this rate we're going to have to provide hotel accommodation as well as hospital beds.'

'That's fair enough,' she smiled. 'Better that way than to have no patients, and the relatives won't expect five-star treatment, I'm sure.'

The child's grandmother got into the car beside Pila and they were off.

As Helen had thought, the requirements of parent and grandparent were extremely simple. They would have been perfectly content to sheep on the floor beside the patient's bed in the brief respites they took from watching and nursing, but Helen helped Thomas to rig up a partition screening off the two empty beds at one end of the ward. The child was put into one and the other was for the resting attendant.

When this was arranged and the young patient comfortable, Helen came into the office to put away the drugs that had come by the aeroplane. A moment later, Colin joined her.

She went on with what she was doing, aware that he was watching from the doorway. 'Did you write up the medication on the chart, Doctor?'

'Yes,' He closed the door and came near to her. 'Helen–' his voice was subdued, 'this is the first chance I've had to talk to you since – since you came for me and I wasn't at home – as I said I would be.'

She stowed away the last of the phials in the cupboard and locked it. 'If the number of patients increases as I think it will when Andrew goes home well, we must have more space for the medicines,' she said in a business-like manner. She turned to him. 'Can you recommend a good handyman? We need shelves and–'

'Let me talk, for God's sake, Helen!' he broke in feelingly. 'It's not going to be easy, but I must try to make you see. I don't suppose you will be able to understand. Life is such a simple uncomplicated business for you, isn't it? Right and wrong, black and white. No compromises.' He pushed his hair back impatiently. 'There I go, starting off to defend myself and ending up attacking you.'

'Do you have to? Defend yourself, I mean,' she asked gently. 'I'm not demanding any excuses or explanations.'

'Oh, no, I daresay you're not! You would rather jump to your own easy conclusions than have to bother digging deeper. I'm a weak character, a drunk and a libertine. That's what everyone else thinks and now you agree with them!'

'Don't be so unfair!' she protested. 'And stop feeling so sorry for yourself. I have tried hard to understand you and to be sympathetic. I was bitterly disappointed when I came for you and found you – drunk, and with that girl!' The time for mincing words was past. 'I did feel – though perhaps I had no right to – I did feel you had let me down. But I didn't condemn you. I still don't. Just because life has been fairly smooth for me so far, and because I was brought up in a rather staid, chapel-going community, does not make me so narrow and prejudiced that I don't realize there are different ways of living that are not necessarily wrong just because they are different.'

They glared at each other for a moment, then Colin's features softened and he said meekly, 'I'm sorry, darling. I know you've tried to see things from my point of view, and you've made allowances for me. You've been much sweeter than I deserve. You were perfectly entitled to feel I'd let you down. I felt the same, and it's such a wretched feeling that I tried to ease it by biting your head off.' He looked so absurdly like a naughty little boy that she couldn't help smiling.

'Sackcloth and ashes don't really suit you,' she told him, but he refused to forgo his self-imposed penance.

'Let me grovel a while longer,' he implored. 'It will be good for my soul.' The lighter mood passed and he went on seriously, 'I must tell you about that afternoon first. I meant to stay home and write my report, honestly I did. But – I don't know,' he shrugged, 'I just couldn't settle down to it. It was so warm and so quiet in the bungalow. I've never been very keen on my own company anyway, and suddenly the place became so oppressive that I had to get out.'

She nodded. 'I think I know what you mean, Colin.'

'Can you possibly?' He was obviously sceptical.

'I told you I'm not so lacking in understanding as you imagine and I think I know what was at the bottom of the way you felt. I–' she hesitated, wondering whether it was wise to put into words what was in her mind, '–but it doesn't matter now.'

'I'd like to hear it and then decide whether it matters or not,' he replied steadily, not meeting her eyes.

She took a deep breath. 'I think you were afraid.' The words came out in a rush. 'You had been working well with me, but after so long – you had been letting things slide rather, hadn't you? – you must have been finding it a bit of a strain. And I guess that you became frightened, unsure of yourself, doubtful as to whether you could keep it up. That was why you went to that hut. There would be no-one there to disapprove or demand. You could get drink there to make things seem better, and–'

'And a woman,' he supplied, as she hesitated. 'Janita.'

'Is that her name? She's beautiful.'

'Yes. She is. And undemanding, as you said.' He looked at her now. 'You're not jealous, are you?' It wasn't a question and it was true.

She said quietly: 'If you were hungry I wouldn't be jealous of the person who gave you food,' and he smiled.

'You're not such a child, after all.' His eyes were gentle. 'Something of a psycho-analyst, too. And you're dead right, my love. I was – still am – scared stiff. All this time other people have been saying I was no good, I smarted under the injustice of it. They were all prejudiced against me for unworthy reasons. But then you came along with your clear eyes and you said I wasn't useless, that I was a good doctor, and that it was up to me to prove this and make others treat me with respect. That was when I began to wonder. Perhaps they were right – the ones who said I was a dead loss. It was possible; more than possible. And on that afternoon I was certain they were. My spirits were at rock-bottom!' He turned away and walked across to the window. Darkness was beginning to fall, and the room was gloomy.

'Shall I light the lamp?' Helen asked.

With his back to her, Colin said, 'Not yet.

162

It's easier to talk when it's like this. Where was I? Oh, yes. In my uncomfortable bungalow, in the heat of the afternoon, trying to concentrate on writing a monthly report, and failing hopelessly, because of this awful depression that came over me. I thought about you, expecting so much of me, and I was sure I could never live up to your ideals. I imagined your disappointment when I let you down, as I knew I would. I couldn't stand it. So I went out. I went to Janita's and got drunk to blot it out of my mind.' He put his hands over his face as if he were still plagued by the disturbing vision, and Helen went to him.

Close, but not touching him, she said comfortingly, 'You don't have to worry about not living up to my expectations now, though. You've proved that you can do it. You saved Andrew's life. No-one could have handled that emergency better, and considering that you are out of practice, you carried it off brilliantly.'

He faced her, studied her searchingly for a long moment, and then grinned. 'I'm pretty damn good really, aren't I?'

'Very damn good,' she laughed, and put her arms round him. There was no passion in their embrace, only affection and comradeship, and Helen said, 'I'll put the light on now.'

As Helen had predicted, the recovery of young Andrew acted as a great inducement to other islanders to come forward for examination or treatment. The child's family, which ran into considerable numbers, had spread the news widely, and in their gratitude had been generous in their praise of the doctor and nurse who had snatched their precious off-spring from the jaws of death. Not only this. They had attempted to repay their debt by offering practical help. Volunteers were forthcoming for the many tasks that urgently needed doing if progress was to continue. The new clinic which had been neglected while Helen was occupied with Andrew had to be thoroughly cleaned and white-washed and simple furniture made for it; extra beds had to be made for the hospital, also shelves and cupboards; Colin's remark about hotel accommodation had to be put into modified effect with the erection of huts for the relatives of patients who came some distance and would have pined if separated from everyone they knew, and above all, perhaps, there was need of nursing aid.

In this connection, two girls came to the

McFarlanes' one morning to offer their services to Helen. Both were related to Andrew and both had been to school. These appeared to be the only similarities, however. One of the girls was plump, with a round face that seemed never to stop smiling, and laughing eyes. She wore a patterned pareu in red and yellow and her hair was twisted into a knot on the crown of her head, held by a red band. Her name was Lia.

The other girl, Salike, was slightly-built and her smooth, black hair fell loosely to her bare shoulders. Her face was small and serious, and when she spoke, her voice was soft and gentle.

The girls waited on the verandah while Meg came to fetch Helen from her room. Having taught them in school, the Scotswoman knew them well, and was able to give Helen a quick briefing.

While the nurse finished dressing and collecting the things she wanted to take with her to the hospital, Meg said: 'I think you could fare a lot worse than take these lassies on. They're both bright and keen, and I found them better at concentrating on a job of work than many of my pupils.'

'That's wonderful,' Helen replied. 'We really need them now.'

'Where had you thought of them living?'

Helen confessed that she had not thought at all about this, and Meg said they would need somewhere nearer the hospital than their village homes. She added, 'Not too small a place either; Lia will need room for her children.'

'Oh. I didn't know she was married.'

'She isn't.' The older woman smiled at Helen's astonishment. 'You're shocked, I suppose, but this bearing of children out of wedlock is not regarded as very terrible here in the islands. A new baby in the family is a welcome event even if its parents are not married. What would be frowned upon would be a girl marrying beneath her, even to legalise a birth.'

Helen looked doubtful. 'I don't know – I can hardly take on a girl with two – illegitimate children.'

'Why not? You'll have to adapt yourself to the island way of life, you know, dear.'

'I know that, but in some things – I mean, if the girl is that type – you said she had two children – it might happen again.'

Meg nodded. 'Aye, it well might. Lia is that type. She's passionate, and a child of nature, despite the thin veneer of sophistication her schooling gave her. No-one has convinced her that it's wrong to follow her instincts and I don't think anyone ever will. I rather hope not. Anyway, I still maintain that she will make a good nurse.'

'But if she's – promiscuous–'

'She is. She is also cheerful, clean and kind, and when she's working her conduct will be beyond reproach.'

The two women looked at each other across an invisible barrier then Helen smiled. 'I'll trust your judgment, Meg. Now, is there anything I ought to know about the other girl? Is she a dipsomaniac or worse?'

'Awa' wi' you,' the Scotswoman laughed. 'No, no. Salike is what she looks; a gentle, quiet, serious-minded gel. She'll give you no trouble.'

Which prophecy proved to be incorrect.

The next week passed busily but without spectacular incident. Young Andrew made steady progress. The wound in his throat had healed and the pneumonia almost gone. A 'Nurses' Home' in the form of a long hut had been erected to accommodate Lia, her two golden-skinned children, a widowed aunt, Salike and a female relative of hers. This was in a pleasant spot a few hundred yards from the hospital. The two island girls were proving quick to learn, and were willing workers. Meg's sewing class had made them caps and aprons which they wore with great pride and laundered enthusiastically at every opportunity. Helen found the girls' passion for cleanliness something of a problem, for they were tireless in their determination to keep not only the wards, but also the patients, as clean as new pins, even if it meant bathing them three times a day. The Welsh girl tried to modify this zeal, but suspected that as soon as her back was turned, the soap and water were produced. There were now ten beds, all filled, and more patients waiting to be admitted as soon as the number could be increased.

Since the cases were not at this time too serious, Thomas was given virtual charge of the hospital. He was thoroughly competent and reliable, and this meant that Helen could spend much of her time at the clinic which was drawing large numbers, mostly of women and babies. Colin visited the hospital every day, but he too took the opportunity of giving attention to patients in their own homes and to the school-clinic he had started.

Being such a valuable asset, Thomas' opinions and reactions mattered a good deal. When he met Lia and Salike his manner puzzled Helen. She had expected him to be pleased at having juniors under his control, but this was not the impression he gave. He was polite; nevertheless it was obvious that as far as Lia was concerned he was less broad-minded than Meg. Perhaps the mixture of his blood had something to do with this. Anyway, he was icily aloof towards Lia, who did not notice and wouldn't have cared if she had.

His attitude to Salike was harder to understand. There seemed to be no reason for disapproval here and yet he treated the young probationer so badly, criticizing everything she did until she was almost in tears, that Helen had to remonstrate with him.

Later, she told Colin of the puzzling affair and was astonished when he offered his explanation. 'He's in love with the girl.'

If this were true, and with a complex character such as Thomas she had to admit it was possible, a number of disturbing questions were raised. In the event of Thomas wanting to marry Salike – or anyone else, come to that – he would have to pay a bride-price. This would be considerable for so desirable a girl, his wage was extremely small.

Oh, dear, Helen thought dismally. Just when things were going so well. If Thomas left the hospital to earn more money, it would be a serious blow to the whole scheme for an improved medical service on the island.

Chapter Thirteen

Helen was afraid of anything happening to upset the smooth routine the hospital had so recently settled into, and the situation developing between Thomas and Salike threatened to do this very thing. At first she had tried to believe Colin's guess was wrong. She watched the couple closely when she was with them, and soon had to admit that, whether they realized it themselves or not, there was a strong feeling of attraction between them. Salike had an admiring devotion to Thomas which she was incapable of concealing; he, on the other hand, had his emotions firmly under control, and betrayed them by the sharpness of his manner towards the girl. He never spoke gently to her or praised her when she did well, but he spent a good deal of time – some of his off-duty – teaching her and explaining to her the many skills a nurse has to acquire. He also kept her occupied in her own off-duty hours with studying, in order, Helen guessed, to reduce the opportunities for her to spend time with, and be influenced by, her colleague Lia.

This state of affairs could not go on. At any moment, a touch of hands, a meeting of eyes, might spark off this smouldering romance. Then the subject of marriage would arise and when that happened the chances of keeping Thomas's valuable services for the hospital were slim. He would have no difficulty in finding better-paid employment, and only the prestige attached to his present job had kept him there until now. If the Medical Commission would increase his salary it would solve the problem admirably.

Helen made a mental note to put the case for an increase in Thomas' pay to Paul Strang when he came again. His next visit was due, she realized. He must be made to see the importance of keeping together the team that had been built up. She had come to depend a great deal on the young Eurasian. She could leave him in charge of the hospital while she gave more time to the clinic. His dependability also enabled Colin to devote his attention to the clinic.

If Thomas left to improve his lot—

Helen's mind was distracted from this problem by the arrival at the hospital of the large white car she recognized as belonging to the Wakefields. She and Colin were on their regular morning visit to the hospital, and were supervising while Thomas demonstrated to the two nurses the task of taking a blood sample, when the car drew up beyond the open ward door.

A moment later, Godfrey Wakefield, in immaculate white suit, appeared in the doorway. 'Excuse me–' he drawled, and Helen went to him. 'It's Anna,' he said. 'She fell down some steps and seems to have hurt herself quite badly.'

'Oh, I'm so sorry. Is she conscious?'

'Good heavens, yes,' he replied ruefully. 'And most voluble, I assure you! The damage seems to be to her leg.'

'Did you examine it to see if there was a fracture?'

He nodded. 'I'm sure nothing's broken. A sprain, I would hazard.'

Helen explained to Colin what had happened and, as they were on the point of leaving for the clinic, he said they would call and see Anna Wakefield on the way. Helen collected the bandages that would be needed if the leg was sprained and went with Godfrey Wakefield while Colin followed in his own car.

Anna Wakefield was lying on a couch in the darkened lounge wearing a pale pink house-coat. She looked up languidly as Helen walked in. She barely glanced at the nurse. Her gaze went to her husband and then past him. 'Where's the doctor?' she asked sharply.

'He's coming,' Helen said, kneeling beside the patient. She moved aside the silk covering. 'It's the left leg, I see. It is slightly swollen round the ankle. Is it painful?'

'Of course it is! I'm sure there's a broken bone.'

Helen felt the joint carefully and then moved it gently. 'Ouch!' the patient objected. 'I think you'd better leave it until the doctor gets here.'

'Very well, though I'm sure there's no fracture.' Helen turned to Godfrey Wakefield. 'We'll probably need cold water – if you could see to that?'

As he left the room, Helen heard the sound of Colin's car. 'Here's the doctor,' she said, and noticed that Anna took a furtive look into the hand-mirror beside her and then watched the door with unmistakable excitement.

When Colin came in, her expression changed. 'You!' she said in disgust.

He grinned. 'Charming as ever, Mrs

Wakefield, even on a bed of pain.' He bent over the couch and ran his fingers over the exposed ankle. 'Some abrasion. No fracture. Possible pulled muscle.'

'You can't be sure,' the patient replied. 'It ought to be X-rayed.'

'Quite unnecessary. I'll strap it up and it will be reasonably comfortable. Rest it for a couple of days. That's all it needs.'

A maid came in carrying a bowl of cold water, followed by Godfrey Wakefield. Colin strapped up the ankle and then stood up.

He said, looking at Helen, 'I might as well have a word with the cook while I'm here. She was operated on for hernia a year or so ago, and needs checking on occasionally.'

He went and Helen asked Anna if she could do anything to make her more comfortable.

The lovely woman on the couch pouted up at her. 'Why isn't Paul here?' she asked frankly. 'It's time for his visit, isn't it?'

Embarrassingly conscious of Godfrey Wakefield's presence in the room, Helen said, 'Yes, it is. But you needn't worry. Dr Fraser is quite capable of taking care of you.'

'Well, I must say he does seem to have pulled himself together lately,' Anna conceded thoughtfully. 'He was always handsome, but had let himself go.' She smiled archly at the nurse. 'Must be the influence of a good woman.' Then the discontent returned. 'But that's not the point. I want to see Paul. I thought he would have been here yesterday. Then I wondered if he might have arrived after dark.'

'I don't suppose he can plan his movements to a day or so,' Helen said. 'Unexpected delays must often hold him up.'

Anna frowned at this. 'You don't think it will be long before he comes, do you?'

'I really don't know, but there's no urgent need for him here at the moment–'

'Oh, isn't there?' Anna spoke under her breath though the words were audible enough.

Deliberately misunderstanding, Helen picked up her case and said cheerfully, 'Your ankle will be all right without any further attention, but I'll come and have a look at it – the day after tomorrow, probably.'

'How kind of you!'

From the far side of the room, Godfrey Wakefield called to his wife, 'Don't sulk, darling. It doesn't suit you,' which did not improve her mood. In fact, her fingers closed around a heavy ornament on the table beside her in such a menacing way that

Helen stepped quickly into the line of fire.

'Well, I must go now. If you have any more trouble with the ankle, ring the McFarlanes. They will know where to get hold of me or Doctor.'

Anna Wakefield stretched her arms above her lovely head and looked at Helen through half-closed eyes. 'Tell Paul Strang the minute he arrives that I want to see him – urgently!' she said with quiet insistence.

Helen smiled politely. 'I'll give him your message.' At the door she turned and said, 'Perhaps when you're up and about again you would like to come down and see the hospital and the clinic.'

As they drove down to the clinic Helen discussed Anna Wakefield's accident and, noting a hint of scepticism in Helen's voice, Colin threw a reproachful glance at her. 'What's this, nurse?' he teased. 'Do I discern a shadow of doubt regarding the lady's fall?'

'Well, I don't mean to be catty–'

'Saints preserve us!' Colin broke in. 'When a woman says–'

'Shut up!' she commanded, giving him a playful slap on the arm. 'It might sound silly, but it wouldn't really surprise me if she had arranged the accident on purpose.'

'But why for Pete's sake? So as to be

attended by me? I hardly think so.'

'No, of course not. She expected Paul Strang to go. She was obviously bitterly disappointed when he didn't.'

He thought this over for a moment and then said slowly, 'You could be right. She would go to greater lengths than that to get what she wanted. And apparently she wants Strang. No accounting for taste, as they say.'

Helen did not reply. She didn't find it difficult to understand Paul Strang's attraction for the lovely, pampered Anna. Her husband gave her everything she wanted in the material sense. She had only to ask and her wish was granted. But the appetite becomes sated and craves the less easily attainable. Helen had known Paul Strang for a very short time, but she felt certain she was right in assuming that so far the relationship between him and Anna was a one-sided affair. This so-called accident appeared to her to be the device of a determined woman; not the act of one who has already achieved her desire.

During the rest of the journey, Helen was quiet. Colin remarked on this and she passed it off lightly. She could not tell him that she was preoccupied by a problem of self-analysis; that, in fact, she was wondering why it mattered so much to her whether or not Anna Wakefield's feeling for Dr Strang was returned.

There was, as usual, a crowd of people waiting outside the clinic, most of them women with babies in their arms or toddlers clinging around the hems of their sarongs. Helen opened the door and went inside the large hut. Here the walls had been washed in pink and she had pinned some pictures, drawn by the schoolchildren, to form a colourful frieze. There was very little furniture. Two tables and a chair and a cupboard. On one table was a weighing machine; in the cupboard, the meagre amount of concentrated fruit juices, processed milk etc, which Helen had to dole out carefully to the many island families suffering from nutrition deficiency.

She went along the patient line of women separating those who needed to see the doctor from the others then, she at one table and Colin at the other, the morning's work went on.

They were almost through when Colin called Helen on one side and said quietly, 'I'm a bit anxious about this woman. From what I can gather she should have been delivered at least a fortnight ago. It's her first child.'

Helen looked beyond him to the girl standing at his table. 'I haven't seen her before, have you?' He shook his head. She asked if he was going to make a thorough examination of the pregnant girl.

'Here? How can I? And the hospital is full, even if it was suitable.'

Helen went to the girl and led her to the only chair in the place. The nurse smiled reassuringly and received a very tired nod of the head in return. Back with Colin she said, 'She looks terribly young, and weary too. What are you going to do?'

Hands in the pocket of his white coat, he looked at the floor. 'I'll see if I can have her taken to Prince Albert Island,' he said. 'She will have the best treatment there. They have the facilities for dealing with cases like this. We haven't.'

'And never will have so long as you keep on sending patients who need special treatment away,' Helen pointed out in a low, but forceful voice. 'The line must be drawn somewhere if things are ever going to improve here.'

'You can't sacrifice this girl and perhaps her child on the altar of your ambition,

180

Helen. I may not be much of a doctor but I wouldn't take risks with a patient for the sake of grinding an axe of my own.'

'I'm not asking you to do that, Colin. Honestly I'm not. I'm thinking of this girl too. She looks to me to be at the end of her tether. And you know the islanders better than I do – how they hate to be separated from their families and villages. She would pine every minute. That wouldn't help her to get well again would it?'

'Oh, Helen–' he sighed. 'I don't know. You're right about her being in a low state. She's under a great strain and I think it's affecting her heart. The journey – with the distress parting from familiar things would cause her – would certainly not help matters.'

'Well, then–' Helen wanted to press home her advantage but at the same time she was anxious not to take the initiative out of Colin's hands. She waited, almost breathless for his reply.

He said firmly, 'I'll give her a thorough examination before I make up my mind. What about taking her to my bungalow? I can telephone from there later, if necessary.'

Helen thought this was a good idea and, when Colin had asked the few remaining women to come back later, they went out to the car. The patient, her name was Kara, was accompanied by an older woman – her mother in law, and a worried-looking young man who was her husband. There was barely enough room in the sports car for Colin, Helen and Kara, so the others had to follow on foot.

While she and Colin were preparing for the examination and before the husband and his mother got to the bungalow, Helen tried to keep up a cheerful conversation so as to prevent tension building up. She remarked that mother-in-law appeared rather stiff in her manner and Colin agreed. He had met the woman before and had found her very much against any change in the traditional ways of doing things. He added that he was surprised she had allowed her daughter in law to come to the clinic and guessed that the son, a strong character too, had put his foot down.

Helen made Kara comfortable on the bed in the spare room and covered her with a sheet. She took the pulse, temperature and blood pressure, wrote them down on a chart, and showed this to Colin. He nodded solemnly as he read the figures.

'Much as I expected,' he said, and proceeded with his examination.

When he straightened up, Helen replaced the sheet, smiling comfortingly at the wide-eyed patient, then she went to Colin. 'Well, what do you think?'

'The foetus is in a very awkward position, a dangerous position possibly,' he told her. 'I wish I could take an X-ray, but I can't so–' He looked at the girl on the bed. 'It's going to be a big baby, far too big for this young woman. I'll turn it and try to deliver it quickly.'

A minute later, with astonished eyes, he put a small brown wriggling body into the towel Helen was holding. And as the thin cry went out from its tiny lungs, he said, 'There's another one, that's the one that's in the breech position.'

Helen held one of the mother's hands tightly and bathed her face as Colin, sweat standing out on his forehead, struggled to bring the second baby into the world. The first, a boy, lay contentedly in the drawer that, padded with a cushion, served as a cradle. Eventually, just as the father and grandmother arrived, panting from their walk from the clinic, Colin held up the second baby, a girl.

The young man glanced at his son and

daughter and then went to bend over his wife. His mother stood in the doorway glaring malevolently at the two babies. Helen noticed this, but was too busy to wonder why or to do anything about it.

'You have a lovely son and daughter,' she said to Kara as she took the patient's blood pressure again. Then remembering that Kara did not understand English, she smiled and pointed to the infants. But there was no answering smile.

The island girl looked terrified, and clung desperately to her husband's hand.

Chapter Fourteen

Helping Colin put the patient comfortable, Helen whispered to him, 'What's wrong? I thought the islanders loved babies. Why aren't they pleased?'

'They love babies,' he muttered, 'but twins – no! They are regarded as an ill omen. They were invariably put out into the forest to die–'

'How horrible! But surely that custom is not still practised? People know better now–'

He shrugged. 'It's like the witch-doctors; it'll take many generations to stamp out completely.'

The woman in the doorway was mumbling angrily to herself, and her son spoke sharply to her. Then Kara began to whimper, and he went over to push his mother firmly into the passage, spoke a few words of command, and closed the door.

The two men talked for a minute and then Colin told Helen that the young father was afraid his mother would try to harm the children. She said, 'They'll have to be watched all the time. That won't be easy here. Do you think it would be better to take the babies somewhere else? To the hospital?'

Colin was doubtful. 'There really isn't room, and they have no time to look after them. The little beggars will have to be protected, though. I wonder if Meg McFarlane could help? She has no love for me, but she is a good-hearted woman in many ways.'

'I'm sure she'll do anything she can. She does have the school to see to–' Helen thought hard for a few seconds, and then said, 'It might work out very well, you know. Let's see – it's about lunch-time. If I go over to the school now we might be able to work something out.'

'Good. I'll show you a short cut from here, as I can't drive you.'

Helen ran all the way. Then after an earnest conversation with Meg hurried back to the bungalow. Seeing the Wakefields' car outside, she thought, 'Oh, dear, Anna Wakefield has sent for me or Colin. Well, she'll just have to wait.' But when she got nearer she saw that Godfrey Wakefield was in the driver's seat, smoking. She didn't stop. Coming into the house, she heard voices, men's voices, angry voices. One was Colin's, the other–

Paul Strang! He was there in the passage

outside the bedroom door with Colin. Both men were silent as she approached, Colin looking as flushed and ruffled as the other doctor appeared cool and calm.

When she had said 'good afternoon' to Dr Strang, she asked after Kara, and the two men had the grace to look a trifle abashed at being reminded that the patient comes before personal feelings.

'She was sleeping peacefully a minute ago,' Colin said.

Helen went into the bedroom, saw that the young mother was still asleep, her husband sitting at her bedside, and the babies were also sleeping. She came out and pulled the door to.

'Can I go and make some coffee, Doctor?' she asked Colin. He nodded, but as she turned to go to the kitchen, Paul Strang said, 'Just one moment, nurse. I want to know exactly what has been going on here since my last visit. So far as I can see, Fraser has been taking a great deal upon himself and I have no doubt he has been aided and abetted by you!' His voice was still quiet, but Helen quailed before his reprimand though she tried not to show it and kept her eyes on his dark face. He went on, 'I must impress upon you, Nurse Davis, that your position here does not entitle you to take charge of the island and that if you continue to act as if it did, you will be exceeding your duties. In that event, I should have to inform the Medical Commission that you were not suitable for the post!'

Before Helen could reply, Colin stepped towards the other doctor and snapped, 'Stop behaving like a pompous bully, Strang! I take full responsibility for everything that has been done here, so you can leave Helen out of this!'

Helen said imploringly: 'Please don't – you'll disturb Kara. Come into the sitting-room.'

After a brief hesitation, the men followed her into the room that was filled with strong early afternoon sunlight. Helen drew down one of the blinds to give some shade and said, 'I'll get some coffee. It won't take a minute.'

When she brought in the tray with drinks and a plate of sandwiches, the doctors were arguing again. She could not help being pleased that Colin was keeping his end up so well. He was putting his point of view in a reasonable way; not losing his temper and blustering as he used to do. She longed to join in and tell Paul Strang what she thought, but with an effort she kept quiet and left Colin to it. She poured three cups of coffee and began to clear a table near a settee for the tray.

Noticing this, Dr Strang said tersely, 'I can't stay. I'm going up to the hospital to have a look at this child Fraser has been practising his kitchen-table surgery on.'

'You'll probably find him sitting out in the garden,' she snapped, as he stalked to the door. 'You didn't have to save Kara or her babies, did you? Dr Fraser handled that case perfectly well.'

He looked at her. 'Childbirth is a natural process.'

'So is breathing,' she countered, 'but lots of things can go wrong with it.'

'I must be getting on,' he said coldly and went out.

'Oh–' Helen clenched her fists, 'I could scream!'

Colin put his arms around her and said gently, 'I know how you feel, darling, but it wouldn't help, would it?'

'Suppose not,' she sighed, leaning against him. 'Anyway, he will come round when he sees the hospital, and Andrew, and everything.'

'I wouldn't count on that. If he's determined to find fault and not to see what he doesn't want to see – well, he'll do just that.'

'Oh, he can't refuse to believe the evidence–'

'You don't know him like I do, my dear,' Colin said grimly, but Helen shook her head.

'I haven't known him as long, but I'm sure he would not be really unfair.' She removed his arms from her waist and went to the coffee table. 'Have a sandwich. I could only find some cheese in a tin to make them with.' He took one and sat down. When she handed him his cup, he looked disparagingly at it.

'I could do with something stronger than that,' he said.

Helen frowned. 'That wouldn't help any more than screaming, would it?' She said it lightly, but inwardly she was saying desperately, 'Oh, please, don't let him start getting drunk. Not now, of all times.' Aloud, she talked about the things they had to do when they had finished lunch. 'Meg is coming to look after the babies as soon as she can leave the school. She's bringing one of the senior girls to help, and when the twins are a bit older she is going to take charge of them while Kara has a good rest. Meg says it will be a good way of teaching babycraft if she takes the twins to school everyday. Isn't she clever?'

'Brilliant!' he agreed laconically, biting into another sandwich.

'Are you going up to the hospital after lunch? One of us ought to be with Dr Strang.'

'Then you'd better go. You appear to understand him so well.'

She put her cup down and passed her hand over her eyes. Not that she felt physically tired; it was a mental weariness that came over her as she wondered if there would ever come a time when life would run smoothly, without these continual set-backs. And she just didn't know how to cope with them. Really, it was a question of people, and the people here – Paul Strang, Colin, Anna Wakefield – were so different from the folk she was used to. Not for the first time she felt an intense longing to be back in dear un-complicated Llandelly again. There had been letters from home yesterday, one from her parents and one from Mair Phillips, full of little incidents that brought the village, the Cottage Hospital, the chapel, so close that it had been difficult to keep back the tears as she read them. Now she took a deep breath and said, 'I can't go yet. I have to see to Kara and the babies, and when Meg comes, I'll have to go back to the clinic. There'll be patients waiting. I'll come up after that.'

He still looked disgruntled, and she came to sit beside him on the settee. 'Colin – don't be like this. We've done so well these last weeks. We must stick together. We're partners, aren't we?'

'Partners,' he repeated heavily, and turned to her. 'Is that all we are now? Working partners?' He took her hand and kissed it. 'You've changed, Helen. I thought you were beginning to love me,' he said huskily. 'God knows why you should, but–'

'I do, Colin,' she told him earnestly. He was right, though. Her feelings had changed. The strong physical attraction he had held for her had passed. She did not tremble at his touch or catch her breath at the sudden sight of him. It must have been what is called infatuation, a thing she had read about but never experienced. There was still affection and he needed her to stand by him if he was to avoid slipping back into the bad habits he had when she came. Believing this she said again, 'I do,' and kissed him warmly on the lips. Then quickly added. 'Now we must get on. Have you had enough to eat? I must give Kara and her husband something. They'll be starving. Where can I get some more milk?'

They stood up and clung to each other for a moment, then parted. Colin said: 'I'll call at the store on my way to the hospital. They'll send it at once. How will you get up there when you're finished here?'

'I hadn't thought about it. Perhaps Angus will bring me in the trap.'

'Lord! That bone-shaker for a five mile journey? No, I'll try to fix something better than that. Wakefield might still be at the hospital.'

'Oh!' Helen exclaimed in horror. 'That reminds me about Anna Wakefield. Did you tell Dr Strang? Or had he been there already?'

'No. Wakefield saw his launch coming in and collected him at the jetty. They went to the clinic first looking for us – Wakefield knew we were heading that way when we left his place – and then came on here.'

'So Dr Strang doesn't know about Mrs Wakefield's sprained ankle? You'd better tell him as soon as you see him.'

'Why? She'll be all right.'

'I know, but we ought to pass on the message. It's up to Dr Strang whether he does anything about it.'

'I'll tell him. If he goes running to the lovely lady all the better. It'll keep him out of our hair.'

Helen turned away. 'How long do you think he'll stay – on the island, I mean?' she asked levelly. 'We must have a serious talk before he goes. There are so many things to discuss.'

'Can't tell,' Colin shrugged. 'It varies from a day to a week. Depends on what there is to do here and how badly they need a doctor on the next island on his list.'

'I see–' Facing him again, she said in a brisk voice, 'Well, off you go. Don't forget the milk.' She steered him to the door and smiled and waved as he went.

It was late afternoon when Godfrey Wakefield came to the clinic to drive Helen up to the hospital. After such a hectic day it was wonderful to relax in his large, comfortable car as it purred along. It would have been easy to fall asleep, and she had to stifle a yawn or two on the way. Arriving on the bustling scene of the hospital precincts, the author parked the car and got out to help Helen out. She thanked him and he bowed over her hand.

'A pleasure, my dear young lady. Now I must get back to my wife.'

'How is she?'

'Oh, better in health than in temper, as the saying goes,' he smiled. 'Poor Anna! She does suffer so frightfully!'

Helen stared at him. 'She does? What's wrong?'

'A complaint more easily diagnosed than treated or cured,' he told her. 'Boredom in its severest form. I have prescribed an interest in something outside herself, but the patient is unco-operative. Of course, she is perfectly justified in quoting to me, "Physician heal thyself", because I freely admit to being the most self-centred of mortals. However–' He gazed around – at the neat garden and paths, the new buildings with islanders moving about them and the grounds cheerfully and confidently – and said, 'I'm greatly impressed by all this activity and also by what I saw earlier at that little clinic of yours.' He patted her hand. 'Come and talk to me about it sometime soon. I might be able to help.'

'That is good of you. Thank you–'

'Not a bit of it!' he declared, indignant at her offer of thanks. 'It should make a good story. Anyway, I've lived on this island for twenty-five years. Lived on it, and lived off it, in fact. It has given me a good hiving, and I've given nothing in return. Perhaps it's time I did.'

Before she could say any more, he was in the car and backing towards the road. She went into the hospital and Thomas came to her.

'Two doctors in office, nurse,' he told her.

She nodded and asked nervously, 'Is everything all right?'

'Patients all comfortable. Nurses Lia and Salike have two hours off duty now.' The young man's smooth face gave nothing away and Helen thanked him and went to the office door.

Hesitating before knocking, Helen heard Colin say, 'I would not have got the job if I was as damn stupid as you think,' and Paul Strang replied icily, 'Family influence! That's how you got it and how you've kept it so long.'

Oh, goodness, should she go in or not? Still wavering, Helen almost held her breath as Colin said, 'Think what you like, but for God's sake – please, Strang, don't tell Helen what happened! Please!'

Chapter Fifteen

She moved hastily away from the door. What did it mean? What was Colin afraid of her knowing? She started nervously as she heard Paul Strang call to her. 'Yes – Doctor?'

'Come into the office, please,' he said.

She took a deep breath and went past him. Colin was not in the office. Dr Strang came in and closed the door. 'Sit down, nurse,' he said in a business-like voice, and sat down himself at the table. He glanced at some papers in front of him, then at Helen.

She thought, he's not as self-assured as usual. For some reason he is uneasy. And he confirmed this frankly.

'I'm in a quandary,' he admitted with a slight smile, and her heart warmed a little towards him. 'Unusual for me. I don't often have difficulty in making up my mind. It's a great help to be rather dogmatic; saves a lot of time. Once you start looking at things from all angles–' he broke off, smiling again, 'but I'm wasting time rambling on like this. I must keep to the point.'

'What is the point, Doctor?'

He leaned back in his chair. 'If I could tell you that, I would not be as confused as I am at this moment. When I came to the island today, I thought I knew what to expect, and had no doubts about how to handle things. As it is–'

'What did you expect?'

'Well, let's say I didn't expect what I found,' he said, sitting forward and picking up his pen. He took off the cap and then carefully put it on again. He repeated this process before saying, 'I didn't expect to see such a change in Colin Fraser. He seems to have grown up suddenly from the irresponsible youth he was only a few weeks ago. The tracheotomy he performed on the child, the delivery of those twins today – they show he has the capability for the job. I was hundreds of miles away when the radio message came through about the emergency operation or I'd have made a dash here. Then I was caught up in an outbreak of cholera. That's why I was a bit late getting here. I need not have worried so much.'

Helen said: 'That's the way it should be, isn't it? We ought to be able to cope with practically anything that occurs.'

'Ideally, yes. But if Victoria is to be

completely self-sufficient medically, you must have a doctor in charge who is utterly reliable.' He looked at her squarely. 'Can you honestly declare that Colin Fraser has that quality?'

She hesitated. 'I think he could have,' she said eventually.

'I don't know. That's why I said I was in a quandary. When I arrived this morning I would not have thought twice; I'd have said bluntly that he is and always will be immature and unreliable. I had grounds for forming that opinion, but perhaps there was some prejudice in it.' He picked up the pen and began playing with it again as he added, 'Is there no prejudice weighing with you, Nurse Davis?'

'I – don't understand what you mean.'

Not taking his eyes off his pen, he said, 'Don't you? I mean that possibly you are allowing personal feelings to influence your judgment. You probably consider it very impertinent of me to interfere with your private affairs in this way. They are certainly no concern of mine – except when they affect your work, or as in this instance, your judgment.'

Helen flushed. 'Yes – well–' she began vaguely, 'I don't know how I can convince you that I'm not – prejudiced – in Dr Fraser's favour. I sincerely believe he could do good work here if he were given the chance.' Then with more spirit, she added, 'You don't have to take my word for it, after all. You have the evidence here in the hospital and in Kara, the girl he delivered of twins today.'

'That's not quite true, my dear. I need more than a handful of cases covering a period of less than a month – I need more than that to go on before I can feel justified in putting a request for a self-contained medical unit for the island to the Commission. I would have to convince them that Fraser would remain in his present state, and first I should have to be convinced myself.'

Hard though she tried to think coolly and constructively; important as she knew this conversation to be, Helen found her thoughts exceedingly wayward. The only one that was really clear in her mind was that he had said 'my dear' to her. Of course it meant nothing. It was no doubt used in a condescending manner. All the same, it stuck obstinately in her brain preventing it from supplying sensible, reasoned arguments as it should be doing. At last she said quickly, 'You must be half convinced or you wouldn't be considering approaching the Commission.'

His face broke into a wide smile, and he looked younger and gayer than she had ever seen him. 'Very astute, nurse,' he said admiringly. 'Yes, I am impressed by what has been accomplished here since you came. I used to regard this as the Cinderella of the Royalties, but now – I was going to say it looks as though the Fairy Godmother had got to work; that would be too fanciful though. There has been a transformation certainly. And I would like to help to put things on a proper basis – if it's going to last.'

'Isn't it worthwhile taking a chance?' Helen asked, leaning forward eagerly. 'There's so much scope here for us. We could do such a lot to raise the standards of the people, given the supplies to work with and the equipment. And after all no one need be any worse off than they are now if it doesn't work out. They can still fall back on the present system if necessary.'

He nodded. 'There is something in that, though the Commission hasn't unlimited resources at its disposal.' He stared pensively at the papers on the table for a moment, then purposefully pulled them towards him and took up his pen once more. 'Anyway, let's get down to brass tacks now. What do you want immediately in the way of supplies? You'll want an increased allocation of baby foods for your clinic, and–'

As they collaborated in drawing up the list, Helen felt so happy that she was afraid. Everything was turning out so unexpectedly wonderful. Her hopes for the island would be realized, now that they had the support of Paul Strang. Paul Strang. He really was not so hard to get on with. Now that he was unbending a little it was quite easy to talk to him.

When the list was completed the doctor stood up and came round the table to Helen. 'If you think of anything else, let me know. I'll be here for another day or so.' He studied her for a moment, and then said, 'It's time you went home, nurse.' He took her hand as she got up. 'I could do with an hour's relaxation myself, so if Fraser will lend us his car I'll drive you to the McFarlanes' and then go on to the Scott's. I'm staying there.'

But as they came out of the office, Godfrey Wakefield came up the ward. 'There you are, Strang,' he called. 'I do apologise for hounding you like this, but Anna–'

Helen gasped. 'Oh my goodness! I forgot–' She looked at Paul Strang in horror. 'I'm awfully sorry, Doctor.'

He looked from her to the other man.

'What's all this about?'

'Mrs Wakefield had a fall this morning,' Helen explained, 'Dr Fraser said she had sprained her ankle, and he bandaged it, but Mrs Wakefield wanted to see you when you got here.'

'I knew about the fall. Fraser mentioned it when he gave me the report. It was a simple sprain, wasn't it? Or is there something else?'

The author was obviously embarrassed as he said, 'No, no, nothing else – physically, as one might say. Perhaps there is a slightly shocked condition– Whatever the trouble, I have no doubt a visit from you would help, Strang. If you could spare the time.'

'I was about to take Nurse Davis home and then go for a bath and a change of clothes. We can look in on your wife on our way.'

When they got to the Wakefield's house, Helen intended waiting in the car. She felt too bedraggled to invite comparison with the always immaculately-groomed Anna. But Godfrey insisted that she go inside for a cool drink, and she gave in.

The 'patient' was now reclining on a long chair on the shady back verandah. Her coppery hair hung loose about her shoulders, and she was wearing a creamy-white satin housecoat. As soon as she saw Paul Strang, her green eyes fastened on him and hardly left him all the time he was there. She said sulkily, ignoring the others, 'So you've come at last. I could have died for all the notice anyone took.'

'A sprained ankle rarely proves fatal,' Dr Strang told her drily. 'How does it feel?'

'Oh, not too bad, I suppose. But you weren't to know that.'

'I knew quite well. Now I must be getting along. I'm keeping Nurse Davis, and she's had a hard day.'

Anna Wakefield sat up to protest and then remembered her delicate condition. Subsiding on to her cushions, she said appealingly, 'Surely you aren't going to dash away already? I've told Cook to prepare your favourite dishes for dinner. She'll be most upset if you don't stay.'

While this conversation was in progress, Helen sipped the drink Godfrey Wakefield had given her and tried to show an interest in what he was telling her about a letter he had received from his publisher. 'My dear, they say that people have seen so much film taken in the South Seas on their horrid little tellys that they're getting tired of the subject.

Disgusting, isn't it? These young fellows scarcely down from university trotting around the world with their cameras and tape-recorders, putting hard-working scribes out of work–'

Helen smiled sympathetically, but her mind was not on the writer's problems. He did not look too worried about his prospects, and she was more concerned with the outcome of the tussle that was being carried on in low voices at the other end of the verandah. Anna Wakefield was obviously used to getting what she wanted and felt confident that she would this time. Helen thought, and secretly hoped, she would not.

So that when Paul Strang came across and asked his host to take her home, adding that he himself had accepted Mrs Wakefield's kind invitation to dinner, she was both surprised and disappointed. And the triumphant smile on the lovely face of Anna Wakefield as they said their goodbyes did not help.

The house was empty when Helen got back to the McFarlanes'. She had a bath, put on a fresh white dress and then, realizing she was hungry, wandered into the kitchen. She found some cooked meat and made herself some sandwiches. Perching on the edge of the table to eat them, she gazed out on to the flower-filled back garden. It was raining. A heavy shower such as often occurred at this time of early evening. Somehow it fitted her mood. Not that it was at all sensible to feel depressed. She had achieved as much as she had dared hope for at her interview with Paul Strang; the future of the hospital and the island as a whole looked bright. She ought to be happy, looking forward, making plans. But she wasn't.

Was it raining in Llandelly, she wondered, and was Mair complaining about it? She would be making plans herself just now for her wedding to David and for their life together on his hill farm. Strange how things work out. Mair, the one who longed to spread her wings and see the world, was happily planning to spend the rest of her life within a few miles of the place she was born in; while Helen herself, who had never yearned for wider horizons, was the one who had come to live at the further end of the earth from everything she knew. She envied Mair the contentment she had found with her good-looking young farmer. How fortunate they were to love and have their love returned.

'Penny for them,' Angus McFarlane's

voice broke in on her reverie, and she smiled as he came in and picked up one of the sandwiches left on the plate.

'Oh, I was just dreaming,' she said.

He nodded. 'Pleasant dreams, I hope, ma dear.' He took a bite of his sandwich and grimaced. 'Ugh! No mustard!' Helen went to the cupboard to get it, and he spread it thickly on his meat as he said, 'Aye, dreaming's a pleasant occupation. No' one you can indulge in verra often, though.'

'There's usually something more worthwhile to do.'

'Maybe, but don't underestimate the dreamers, the visionaries of the world. They have their part to play, too.'

'Yes, but it's time I did some work again. I must go and see how Kara and her babies are. Your wife is with them just now.'

'Aye, I heard the news on ma travels, and looked in for a few minutes. Meg told me of the mother-in-law's reaction. I wasna surprised, of course. I knew the old belief still had its adherents, but all the same it is discouraging, when one has worked for a quarter of a century spreading the gospel of God's love, to find that the powers of darkness prevail. Perhaps in trying to avoid the mistakes of my predecessors, I've been too permissive. They expected natives to conform immediately with their own strict standards; they banned dancing so there was no artistic self-expression, and they were fanatically determined to cover the nakedness that was far cleaner and healthier than the hideous garments they forced on the poor islanders.' He grinned apologetically. 'I'm afraid I got on to my hobby-horse then, but you see what I'm getting at, don't you?'

Helen said: 'Yes, I think so. Yours is the right way to get progress, even if it takes a long time. We have problems of this kind too, you know. Apart from this fear of twins, the medicine man still has a big influence on the people. It isn't always bad, though. The other day a woman brought a child to the clinic; it had a skin complaint. The ointment I gave her didn't help, but some time later she brought the youngster back – cured. She told me she'd used a remedy her mother had learned from a witch-doctor, banana juice mixed with cow's milk. I'll remember that when a similar case crops up, because the child's skin was perfect the last time I saw him. So it's not always a one-way traffic in knowledge. Sometimes they can teach us.'

'Oh, there's no doubt the witch-doctors

mixed a certain amount of folk-medicine knowledge with their fetishes and taboos. It's when the power of fear holds these people back that we must stamp on it as hard as we can. These twin bairns must be protected at all times.'

'They will be, Angus. The young parents will have no truck with ancient customs, and they'll see no harm is done.' Helen went to the window. 'The rain is stopping. I'll get a jacket and go along to take over from Meg.'

'I'll take you there,' Angus said, going to the sink to swill his face with cold water.

Colin was at the bungalow, rather peeved that Helen had left the hospital without saying anything to him. She told him about Godfrey Wakefield's call and said that, not knowing where Colin was, it seemed better not to lose time looking for him. To this he replied huffily that he had not wished to interrupt her long chat with Strang and had gone to supervise the gardeners for a while.

'Well, is everything all right here?' Helen asked. 'I'd better let Meg know I'm here, then she can get home. Angus brought me here; he'll be waiting on the verandah to take her back.'

Meg assured Helen that all was well. Mother, father and babies had recently been fed and were comfortable. Helen thanked her for her help and walked to the door with her.

'I'll bring a few things to make this place a bit more homely tomorrow,' the Scotswoman said. 'It's fairly given me the creeps to spend an afternoon in such a discomfortable house. Ma own's no' the last word in luxury, I know fine, but– Och, well, the puir lad canna be expected to do woman's work or keep a maid on her toes.'

Helen watched the pony and trap chip-chop away into the darkness and marvelled at the sympathetic tone in which the older woman had referred to Colin. He was a 'puir lad' now, was he? She went into the sitting-room and Colin asked what she was smiling about. 'Was I smiling? It was something Meg said – about you,' she said mysteriously.

He looked dubious. 'I don't suppose I would find it funny. I know her opinion of me.'

'I think it's changed a little,' she said, sitting down on the settee. 'In fact, any minute now she is likely to start mothering you.'

'Heaven forfend!' he entreated, chapping a hand dramatically to his brow. 'I think I prefer her acidity to sweetness and light. I can see it now – wee bowls of nourishing broth, my socks whisked away to the wash, bunches of flowers all over the place!'

'Why not? You need taking in hand.'

'Do I?' He looked down at her, seriously now. 'Perhaps you're right.' Suddenly he dropped down on to the settee beside her and grasped her hand tightly. 'What about applying for the job yourself?' he asked hoarsely.

'Me?' She swallowed hard. 'Oh – I can't make broth – and I'm not much good at washing socks,' she said lightly, though inside she was in a turmoil. She stood up quickly and pulled her hand away. 'I could tidy up a little. Look at this desk of yours!' Crossing to a littered bureau, she began by emptying a filled ashtray into a waste-paper basket. Then she picked up some loose papers. 'Have you a folder these could go into?'

'There'll be one in the drawer, I suppose,' he said without interest, and took out his cigarettes.

Helen opened the top drawer and lifted out the contents. 'I expect most of this is stuff that could be thrown out,' she said. 'You don't want this old magazine, do you? And–'

'What's the matter?' he asked as she broke off. She didn't answer. She was staring at a photograph that had slipped out of the magazine. A photograph of a laughing girl with long auburn hair. And written across the picture were the words, 'With love, Gina.'

She knew that Colin had come to look over her shoulder, but she did not move or speak. Gina. Georgina. With love. An accident. Killed at once. 'Don't tell Helen–' Slowly she turned to him.

'Don't look like that, Helen,' he pleaded. 'It doesn't mean anything.'

'Doesn't it mean that Georgina was in love with you? And that she took her life because of it?' she asked in a flat voice.

'I don't see how you make all that out of a photograph! "With love" is something everybody puts on photos. Anyway, who told you she killed herself?'

'No-one. I asked Meg what happened to Nurse Grey and she told me she'd fallen – an accident. But it wasn't, was it? Did she wear her hair loose when she was on duty?'

'Did she–? No, she wore it pinned up. What on earth–?'

'It was loose when they found her. If she was not working why should she be anywhere near the cliff ledge?'

He did not speak.

'Tell me the truth, Colin,' she said quietly.

Chapter Sixteen

He met her eyes for a moment and then glanced at the photograph still in her hand. 'All right. I didn't want you to know, but since you do I might as well fill in the details.' He drew on his cigarette and then stubbed it out in the ash-tray on the desk. 'Gina did kill herself. She was a strange girl in some ways. That ledge in the cliff used to fascinate her. I often found her sitting out there, looking down at the rocks and the sea thousands of feet below. I warned her of the danger if she lost her balance, but she just laughed. I'm not trying to make excuses for myself when I say she was slightly unstable. I knew she was in love with me. I took her around a bit, but she was – well, not my type. Rather immature. And I never pretended to feel anything more than friendship for her. I was sure she'd get over it. But she didn't. She was terribly jealous – of Janita. It never occurred to me that she would do what she did, though. I was staggered. She walked – or ran – all the way up to the hospital.' He put his hands over his face. 'They found the remains of her flimsy shoes on the road, and her feet were bloody and dirty when she was discovered. That was when I started drinking heavily – to try to stop myself thinking about that girl's broken body lying on those rocks. It didn't help much. Neither did it help to know that other people were blaming me for driving her to it. I suppose you do now.' He turned away and went to the cupboard where the drinks were kept. He put a hand out to turn the key, then drew it back and walked to the settee where he sat wearily down.

Helen watched him for a minute, then went and poured him a glass of whisky. He accepted it with surprise and gratitude.

Neither spoke until he had finished the drink. Helen took the glass and asked if he wanted any more. He hesitated for an instant before shaking his head. 'No. No more, thanks.'

'I – I'm sorry, Colin,' she said softly.

He looked up at her, puzzled. 'What have you to be sorry for?'

'For making you talk about – what happened. It must have been awful for you.'

'You don't think it was my fault then? That I drove her to it?'

216

'No. I don't think you were to blame – if you've told me the truth.' He swore that he had, and she went on, 'It's a terrible thing to have happened. The poor girl – But you couldn't know she would do such a thing. Unrequited love. It's – tragic. It can't be helped, though. No one can demand that the one they care for should feel the same about them.' Helen was talking almost as if to herself, standing in the dimly-lit room. 'The miracle is when two people do love each other equally. And miracles don't often happen.'

Colin reached out to take hold of her hand. 'No, Helen dear, most relationships are based on compromise, those that are at all lasting anyway.' He drew her down to the settee beside him and put his arm lightly round her shoulders. 'Suppose we stop talking in generalities and get to us.'

She stiffened a little. 'Not now, Colin. I must go and see to my patients,' she said unsteadily.

His arm tightened so that she could not get up. 'The patients are fine, nurse. It's the doctor who is in need of attention,' he told her, smoothing her hair tenderly back. 'It's true, darling. I need you so much. You know that, don't you? You're so sweet, so understanding–' He kissed her cheek, her temple, and turned her face to his, 'Darling–'

'No–' Helen bent her head, and his hold slackened.

'What's the matter? Have you changed so much, in such a short time?' His tone was still gentle, and she didn't move away from him.

'I don't know, Colin. I think I must be what my mother calls impressionable.'

'So is everyone when they're young and inexperienced. Where do we go from there?'

'Well, you were so different from the men I met at home,' she answered, flushing, 'I was attracted.'

'Mutual, I'm sure,' he smiled.

'That isn't love, is it?'

He shook his head. 'No, physical attraction isn't love, whatever the popular songs would have one believe.' He paused, then asked, 'Was that all you felt? Is there nothing left?'

She looked thoughtfully at him. His eyes were brown with specks of gold in them, and they were soft and slightly fearful. Unbidden came the thought, Paul Strang's eyes are much darker, almost black, and never afraid. 'I still care for you, Colin,' she said sincerely. 'I don't know much about love. I

218

love my parents; I love North Wales. I can understand those kinds of loving. But I have never felt strongly about a man – not before I came here.'

'Dear little Helen, I'm so glad you still care; more glad than you can know.' He took her face in his hands and kissed her lips. She put her arms round him and returned his kiss warmly, holding him, comforting him. He caressed her neck affectionately and said, 'I think you know quite a lot about loving. I've never met anyone like you, darling. You're all a man could ever want. Oh, Helen, Helen, I know I've no right to ask you, but please say you'll marry me!'

She closed her eyes, leaning against him as a haphazard jumble of thoughts raced through her mind. This was not the way a girl ought to feel on receiving a proposal. She knew that. But as Colin had said, most relationships that last are a compromise. It was not essential that both partners should be deeply in love before they could make a successful marriage. And when they were partners in more than one sense. They would be working together in an important cause, and that would be a strong bond. 'Yes, Colin,' she said firmly, 'I will marry you – if you really want me.'

'If I really–?' He raised her head to look at her in wonder and delight. 'Darling, do you mean it? I can hardly believe it. God knows I don't deserve such luck. Oh, Helen–' He kissed her again, then, his face still very close to hers, whispered, 'I'll try to make you happy. I swear it.'

'And I'll try to be all you want me to be, Colin,' she vowed.

'This certainly calls for a celebration,' he declared, jumping gaily to his feet. 'Only in wine, though. I've got a decent bottle tucked away somewhere.'

They raised their glasses.

'To us,' Colin said happily.

'To us,' Helen repeated, gripping her glass hard.

It was late when Colin took her home that night. She had made a meal for Kara and her family and settled them down for the night, then got supper for herself and Colin. While they ate, they discussed the changes that seemed likely now that Paul Strang had promised at least limited support, and Colin had laughed and said, 'I don't suppose many couples have spent the first evening of their engagement talking about penicillin and D.D.T.

The drive home in the cool, bright moonlight was restful. It was so quiet that the sound of the car wheels on the coral road seemed more than usually noticeable. 'Tired, darling?' Colin asked.

'Mm – a little,' she sighed, and leaned her head on his shoulder. 'It's been quite a day.'

He bent to plant a kiss on her hair. 'It certainly has, darling. Quite a day!'

They said goodnight under the frangipani tree at the front gate, and then Helen ran up the path and into the house. She saw no-one on her way to her room.

After a restless night, she slept rather late and only had time for a few words with Meg next morning before rushing out to meet Colin who had come to take her to tend Kara and family. As soon as they were on their way, he asked if she had told Meg and Angus the news.

'About us, you mean? No, I haven't had a chance.'

'Of course I mean about us, my pet,' he laughed. 'So they don't know yet?'

'I didn't see anyone last night, and it was a rush this morning to get ready.'

He gave her a shrewd side-long glance. 'You're not afraid to tell them, are you? I know the Mac's aren't particularly fond of me, even if their hearts have softened slightly of late.'

'Of course I'm not afraid,' she assured him, and he smiled.

'All right, darling, but we will tell them together if you'd rather.'

They drove in silence for a minute or two, then Helen asked if the babies had kept him awake. 'No, all my lodgers slept very well. The twins yelled for food at three o'clock but they soon settled down again.' He frowned at some recollection and Helen questioned him. 'It's nothing much, but when I was going back to bed after putting the babies back in their cots I looked out of the window. I might have been wrong, but I saw a figure lurking in the bushes just beyond my garden and I thought it was the old mother-in-law.'

'Oh, Colin, do you think she means to harm the twins?'

'I'm sure she would if she got the chance. We'll have to see she doesn't get it.'

When they came within sight of the bungalow, Helen began to peer anxiously ahead. There was a coconut palm grove on one side of the road and many trees and bushes to afford cover for anyone seeking it, and she could discern no movement or shadow to rouse suspicion. 'I don't know how anyone can be afraid of two new-born babies,' she said, as Colin pulled up at the house.

He shrugged. 'If you believe that evil spirits can enter the human body and that they favour twins as a vehicle, it's not so strange, I suppose.'

They went into the hall and Helen caught a glimpse of a woman through the open kitchen door. The figure disappeared quickly and she touched Colin's arm. 'There's someone in the kitchen,' she whispered urgently.

'That's only Kiki, my housekeeper. She's sparing me an hour or two today from her main job of looking after her large family.' He smiled and patted her shoulder. 'I oughtn't to have told you about seeing that suspicious character. Now you'll be looking over your shoulder all the time. She won't try anything in daylight, and I don't think she'll attempt to do actual harm now. Obviously she hasn't been able to stir up support among the islanders. They are too enlightened, except for the scattered few.'

'What would they have done – if many thought like her?'

'Taken the babies into a remote part of the forest and left them to die.'

Helen shuddered. 'How horrible!'

'But that's not going to happen. If the old woman had a chance of rousing the people's emotions, of working up their fears, those youngsters wouldn't be yelling for food at this minute.'

'I must go and see to them. Is there plenty of milk? Good. Meg's coming over straight after morning school to take charge for a couple of hours so that– What's that?' She turned towards the front door as it was pushed back.

Paul Strang stepped into the hall. 'Good morning, nurse – Doctor. I thought I'd look in to make sure all is well.'

Helen said, 'Good morning, doctor. I was just going to prepare the babies' feed – if you'll excuse me,' and hurried into the kitchen.

There, she stood quite still, with her eyes tightly closed. I'm going to marry Colin, she told herself. But I don't love him. Not as I should love the man I marry.

The man I love is Paul Strang!

Chapter Seventeen

As she went automatically through the motions of preparing food for the babies, Helen wondered if it was always like this. When a person fell in love; really in love. If it always hit you with such force, 'this is the one', that you were helpless before it. She was going to marry Colin; that was an unalterable fact. He loved her and needed her if he was not to fall back into the bad habits of a short time ago. She was fond of him, and could have faced the future quite happily but for this – this–

Just managing to snatch up the pan from the flame before the frothing milk boiled over, she pulled herself together. She had work to do.

She tried to keep out of Paul Strang's way as she went about her tasks of feeding and bathing and bedmaking, hoping he would not be staying long at the bungalow. But when everything was done he was still there. He was talking to Colin in the sitting-room when she came from the bedroom Kara and the babies were using.

'All settled comfortably,' she announced brightly, glancing from one doctor to the other. Had Colin told Dr Strang of their engagement, she wondered. She thought not, and was glad. She needed a little while to adjust to the situation before she could face receiving congratulation from the man she loved on her intended marriage to someone else.

She fidgeted around straightening cushions for a minute or so then asked Paul Strang if she could make him coffee before he left.

'Are you trying to get rid of me, nurse?' he said, and smiled at her embarrassment as she denied the suggestion. 'All right. But don't bother with coffee for me, please. I am going now. Will you come up to the hospital with me?'

'Oh – I don't think I can leave until Meg – Mrs McFarlane gets here to keep an eye on things.'

Colin said innocently, 'That's O.K., I'll hang on for an hour or so. I have some paper work to catch up on.'

There was nothing for it but to say, 'Very well, I'll get my case,' and to submit.

Paul Strang went outside to turn the car – borrowed from his host – and Colin came to put his arms round Helen. 'What's wrong, darling?' he asked gently. 'You seem a bit edgy – particularly with Strang. You don't dislike him that much, do you?'

'There's nothing wrong,' she told him, putting her cheek against his.

'Sure? I know he's a big-headed individual, but he'll be leaving this evening. Then we'll have peace for another month.'

'You didn't tell him – about us?'

'No. He wouldn't be interested in our little private concerns.'

'I suppose not,' Helen moved away, patting her hair into place. 'He is an important man, after all. I'd better not keep him waiting. See you soon.'

Paul Strang's first remark as he drove along the flame-tree-lined road was, 'We'll call on Anna. It's not out of our way.'

Helen looked at his dark profile. It gave nothing away. No hint of his feelings for Godfrey Wakefield's lovely wife. He admired her beauty, that much was obvious. No man could fail to do so. But how much more than admiration was there in his regard? Impossible to guess. Anyway, what did it matter? It could not affect Helen whether he was in love with Anna Wakefield or not. But oh, it did matter. And it did affect her. She couldn't bear to think of his caring for the other woman; yet reason told her that few men would be proof against such a desirable prize that was so clearly theirs for the taking.

Unconsciously, she sighed deeply and was surprised when he asked her if she was tired. She said perhaps she was, a little, and was grateful that he did not attempt to keep up the conversation. She leaned back and watched the road until the dazzling glare of it in the morning sunlight made her chose her eyes.

She opened them with a start when the car stopped, and saw the Wakefields' house gleaming whitely before her. This time she did not get out of the car. Paul Strang had said there was no need, he would only be a minute, just long enough to check that the sprained ankle was giving no trouble.

Helen said meekly, 'Very well, Doctor,' and stayed where she was. She was glad to. Then as the minute stretched to two – three – four – five, she began to chafe. Anna Wakefield would be using her considerable charm to keep Paul there. Perhaps he did not need much persuasion.

A moment later, Paul Strang came on to the verandah carrying Anna easily in his arms. He bent to put her on a long basket chair but her arms clasped about his neck did not let go. Helen was close enough to hear the tinkle of provocative laughter as the other woman teased the solemn-looking doctor until he laughed too. A sharp pang of jealousy stabbed through Helen and she looked away.

When Paul Strang re-joined her, there was still an amused expression on his dark face, and she could not resist saying with mild sarcasm, 'I hope the patient is quite comfortable, Doctor?'

At the hospital, Thomas had the morning's work efficiently under way. The ward, now divided into two by a partition, was tidy and clean; the patients were mostly sitting up in their narrow beds wearing freshly-laundered white shirts or gowns, and the nurses bustled swiftly about.

Helen went from bed to bed, as Dr Strang had a word with each patient, and as she did so, became increasingly aware of a slight tension in the atmosphere. She tried to put her finger on the root of it, but it was not until the round was finished and she went to thank Thomas for taking charge that morning, that she realized where the trouble lay.

In reply to her congratulations on the way the hospital looked he merely grunted. Usually he lapped up praise, beaming all over his face. Why not today? 'Is something worrying you, Thomas?' she asked kindly.

At first she thought he was not going to answer. His face had a 'closed-up' expression she had never seen before. Then he said in a flat voice, 'I cannot stay at the hospital, Nurse.' He spoke slowly and deliberately, for some of the words were difficult for his half-Polynesian tongue to produce and his pride prevented his pronouncing them incorrectly. The result was an air of finality that left Helen speechless for a second.

Eventually she managed to ask the reason for this decision, and learned that the young man wished to obtain more lucrative employment in order that he might raise the bride-price required by Salike's father. So she had been right. This was what she had feared would happen and had meant to discuss with Paul Strang.

'Don't do anything in a hurry, Thomas,' she said. 'You have not known Salike very long, have you? I will talk to the doctor and see if he can do anything.'

The young man agreed to wait a little before seeking other work and went off for his mid-day meal.

Helen watched him thoughtfully. If Thomas did leave the hospital he would be badly missed. Without him to take charge, Colin or herself would have to spend much more time there, with consequent neglect of their other work. The progress they hoped for would be almost impossible to achieve.

She went into the office. Paul Strang was there with a tall man she recognized as the father of Andrew, the 'tracheotomy boy'. The islander was chattering excitedly and Paul interpreted. 'I've told him he can take Andrew home now, and he's inviting us to a party to celebrate the lad's recovery. I gather it's to be quite an occasion.'

'It sounds exciting,' Helen smiled. 'When is it to be?'

'This very evening. It's all been planned and prepared for weeks, just waiting for the boy to be discharged.'

'This evening! You'll miss it, then, won't you? You'll have left Victoria.'

'Oh, I can't miss such an occasion! I'll stay on for an hour or so, anyway. I don't often get the chance of experiencing a slice of genuine island life these days.' There was a wistful note in the doctor's voice. Clearly, he felt regret that with the advance of modernisation, the old cultures and traditions were being lost.

This attitude in him rather surprised Helen. She would have expected him to regard the old ways as bad ways, and to be all for change and progress. It proved that there was much about him that she did not yet know.

Andrew's father went to see his son and collect his few belongings prior to being taken home, and Helen had her opportunity to speak to Paul Strang about Thomas.

The doctor listened intently, hands in the pockets of his white coat, staring at the floor, and when she had finished stating her case, he remained so for a moment or two. Then he looked at her thoughtfully. 'I can understand that you don't want to lose the services of this young man, nurse.' he said slowly, 'and the payment he's getting now is really inadequate. But we are working on a very tight budget; our money has to go a long way; and I still am not sure I would be justified in recommending the Commission to take on extra expense here.'

Helen protested: 'But you said when we talked yesterday that you would improve things on the island!'

'I said I would increase your supplies and

I am giving serious consideration to the other points we discussed,' he told her, and she reflected that he was a different person from the man of only a moment ago. Now he was solemn and formal again. He went on, 'but I've still got doubts. I haven't made any decision about making large-scale changes here. I hope I didn't give you a false impression.'

'I – suppose it was a bit of wishful thinking,' she admitted, unable to conceal her disappointment. What could she say to sway him? If she had failed to convince him yesterday when she could talk calmly and dispassionately, what chance had she now that her mind was filled with the new and overwhelming awareness of her love for the man standing near her. Near, and yet how far away.

'You see the difficulty, don't you nurse?' he asked, 'I have to decide – I'll be quite frank with you – whether this "New look" you've created here is something that will last, or whether it's a flash in the pan; a case of a new broom sweeping clean.'

She looked at him, then away. Took a deep breath and said slowly, 'Would it help you to make up your mind if I told you that Dr Fraser and I are going to be married?'

He said nothing immediately and she could not refrain from glancing at his face. The news had apparently come as no surprise to him. Other than that she could not gauge his reaction. When he offered formal congratulations, his voice was completely expressionless. Then be said, 'This could make a difference. A marriage between you and Fraser would tend to stabilize the situation.' Goodness, Helen thought, he sounds as if it was a treaty between two countries he was talking about. Never mind, though, if he did come around to her way of thinking on the main point – the future of the island – nothing else mattered.

A tap on the door interrupted the discussion. It was Thomas to say that Andrew and his father were ready to leave. Dr Strang was to drive them home and he went to the door, turning to tell Helen that he would not be long, before going out.

Music, laughter, colour and wonderful food. That was what the celebration was made up of that evening, with a few moments of quiet when halting, emotional words of thanks were addressed to Colin and Helen for bringing young Andrew through his serious illness. The boy, bursting with health and self-importance, sat at one end of a long table that was laden with dishes of foods mostly unfamiliar or in strange guises. She and Colin were at the opposite end, with relatives and friends between. The table stood on a clearing in the village centre under huge ironwood trees and the moon shone brightly on the gay scene. There was poi, made from bananas, breadfruit, paw paw; there were ripe bananas baked and green bananas boiled; there was mango salad; rounds of taro, floury inside with hard brown crusts, raw prawns in fresh lime juice with coconut cream, curried goat with rice, tiny dishes of sea-eggs – all so delicious that Helen soon forgot her qualms about island cookery. She blithely wiped her platter with a piece of taro to receive a thick slice of pork from the sucking pig that had been roasted whole before her eyes, and wiped it again ready for the next course.

Of course, a large crowd of curious islanders had gathered to watch the fun and all were made welcome, drink and food being handed around liberally, and when everyone had eaten and drunk the table was moved away to make room for dancing. Helen was glad to sit and watch and listen to the music, while she recovered from the meal. Colin was beside her. Once or twice he got up to join in a dance, to the great delight of the islanders.

The evening's festivities were at their height when a white car drove up and Paul Strang got out. Helen thought, this is the last time I'll see him for a month. It will seem an endless stretch of days. Would her feelings change in the course of it? When he returned would she be able to look at him without this yearning ache in her heart; would she be able to hear his voice with no start of emotion? She knew the answer. No, no, no. This was not a passing infatuation. This was love, and would grow and deepen, not diminish. She wanted to get up now and go to him, just to speak to him for a moment, but the noisy jostling people crowding between made this difficult. Besides, if he wanted to talk to her, he would get through. He smiled and waved at her and Colin, remaining on the edge of the crowd.

Helen tried to enjoy the proceedings and forget her own concerns, but when she noticed Paul Strang looking at his watch, she thought, he will be going soon. I won't even be able to say goodbye. More and more people swarmed around, the noise grew louder and the heat from the open fire more intense, so that she became dazed by it all and closed her eyes. The noise began to recede further and further until it was a faint moaning in her ears and then there was a strange pitiful sobbing. She opened her eyes and it was she who was sobbing, her face against Colin's shoulder, his arm comfortingly around her. 'Goodness, I – I'm sorry–' she stammered in confusion, but he smiled.

'It's all right, darling. You're tired out, aren't you? I'll make our excuses and take you home. This party will go on for hours yet.'

They stood up and Colin shepherded her carefully through the throng, explaining as he went that 'Miss Nurse' was tired now, but had had a wonderful evening.

When they reached the fringe of the crowd, Helen looked from side to side, but there was no sign of Paul Strang or the car.

The days passed, not unhappily, for Helen. She worked hard, and the satisfaction she got from doing a worthwhile job made up in large part what she was lacking in her private life. Colin was working as hard as she, and every day seemed to gain confidence and stature. They built up a partnership based on respect and affection, which Helen told herself was a good foundation for marriage. After all, one cannot have everything. And if there was a persistent ache in her heart for something more – well, she would just have to make the best of it.

Meg McFarlane had received the news of the engagement with no great pleasure, but she had conceded that 'perhaps it will work out better than maybe.' She began to invite Colin to dinner two or three times a week, and Helen could see her being gradually won over by his gay friendliness and by his obvious love and solicitude for Helen. One night when, as often happened, she came into Helen's bedroom with a hot drink and to have 'a wee chat', she had talked about him. 'I can see now that I've been rather hard on the young man,' she had said, smoothing Helen's counterpane and then sitting on the edge of the bed, hands clasped round her thin knees. 'You see, Angus and I were very fond of Georgina, and when she died – you know all about it the now – well, we were upset, of course. We, especially me, blamed Colin. That was unfair. It was not his fault. Gina was a sweet girl, but not a strong character, I'm afraid. She was excitable, even on occasion to the point of slight hysteria, and a thing that another girl would have got over – disappointment in love – was too much for her mind to take. A terrible tragedy. If the fault can be laid at any door, it would be the Medical Commission's, for sending her out here away from family and friends who might have prevented such a thing.' The Scotswoman had sighed and shaken her grey head. 'A sad affair entirely, but love can't be ordered. It happens, or it doesna', and that's all there is about it.'

And Helen had echoed the sigh.

Chapter Eighteen

One morning when she ran down the path to where Colin was waiting in his car to drive her to the hospital, she saw an official-looking envelope in his hand. She got in beside him and took it from him. It was from the Medical Commission and she saw with a pang that it was signed by Paul Strang in a firm, clear hand. It said that it had been agreed that Thomas Jones be awarded an increase in salary; also put the employment of Lia and Salike on a proper footing, and said that a full report on the discussions held during his recent visit to Victoria Island had been submitted to the Board of Commissioners, together with his own recommendation.

Arriving at the hospital, they could tell at once from his beaming face that Thomas had also had a letter. This thanked him for his services to the hospital as well as informing him of the rise in pay. 'You will stay with us now, won't you, Thomas?' Helen asked, and he nodded happily.

'I not ever want go, Miss,' he said, his excitement doing his English no good at all.

That same day, Godfrey Wakefield had come for a 'look round' the clinic and as he left, handed a cheque for a substantial amount to Helen. 'Most praiseworthy, my dear, what you're doing,' he had said. 'but this might provide a little comfort.'

So Helen was able to plan cubicles with pretty curtains and floor coverings and a play ground for the toddlers, in her few spare moments.

Physically and mentally she was working all out, yet never a day went by without her thinking, another twenty-four hours nearer to Paul Strang's next visit. It was no use telling herself to stop thinking about him; she had tried to put him out of her mind many times without the least success.

She did manage to preserve an appearance of calm, even happiness. Until the day he was due to arrive and he did not come. She said nothing to anyone to indicate that she knew he was overdue. It was not unusual, after all. His last visit had been late, and there was no urgent need for his presence. Only her need.

The next day passed and still he did not come. She remarked on it as casually as she could to Colin as he drove her home after an evening visit to Kara and her babies. He nodded. 'I don't know what's holding him up this time, unless he's been caught in that freak hurricane.'

Helen turned to him. 'Hurricane? But this isn't the time of year for them, is it?'

'No. We don't normally get them till November at the soonest. Once in a while, though, one suddenly blows up from nowhere and hits us. And I heard over the radio early this morning that there was a freak heading this way. It was reckoned to strike the outer Royalties at about noon today.'

Oh, God, thought Helen clenching her hands hard, and him in a small boat that could be dashed to pieces by a gale, let alone a hurricane. 'The – outer Royalties,' she repeated dully.

'Yes, Charlotte and Caroline islands.'

'And that's where – Dr Strang – would be?'

'Well, that would be his usual schedule – to call at those islands immediately before coming here.'

Helen bit her lip. This was dreadful. To be so afraid and so afraid of showing it. Yet somehow she must know what was happening. She said quietly, 'Can we find out – radio a message to one of the other islands–?'

'There may be a call now at the station,' Colin replied. 'I intended going in on my way home–'

'Let's go now. Please.'

'All right, darling.' He patted her hand and smiled. 'Don't look so anxious. The hurricane might have blown itself out in the ocean before it got to the islands, and anyway, with due warning, there wouldn't be too much danger. In fact, the islanders welcome them in a way, because they leave a harvest of blown down coconuts and stranded fish and crabs to be collected.'

'Yes, I suppose so,' she said without conviction. She knew that a hurricane force wind could uproot a palm tree easily; what then would it do to the small boat Paul travelled in? This was the question that kept pounding in her brain, and pictures of the craft being smashed against jagged rocks tormented her so that she hardly knew what she was doing.

When they got to the radio station, she had the car door open and had jumped out before Colin could get round to help her. They went into a communications room where a middle-aged, bespectacled man took off head-phones to greet them. In answer to Colin's enquiry, he said in a slow voice with a New Zealand accent, 'No, Doc, no incoming calls for you. I've tried three times to raise one of the outer Royalties, but it's no go.'

Colin nodded. 'Get through to Prince Albert, Ted, and find out what's happening with the hurricane.'

He got a chair for Helen and she sat down, her hands clasped together in her lap, her face pale and set. Her mind was a blank now and she just waited passively for news, unaware of voices or movement around her. When Colin put his hand on her shoulder, she started, as if out of sheep. 'What – what is it?'

'Nothing much, darling. Princess Charlotte Island caught the main force of the hurricane and we can't make direct contact, so we have no details of the damage yet.'

Helen looked up at him and tried to speak, but nothing came. How could she say what she longed to say? All she could do was to pray, 'Oh, God, let him be safe. Please, please, keep him safe.'

Colin said: 'Come along, I'll take you home.'

'No, I'd rather wait.'

'But there may be no more news before morning, dear. I'll stay here, and telephone you as soon as we get anything definite.'

'Let me wait a little longer, please Colin.'

He looked around the bare functional room and then asked the operator if he could take Helen into the next room where there was a comfortable chair, and was told to do so, by all means.

When she was settled in an easy chair, Colin pulled out another up for himself and took out his cigarettes. He offered her one, and she took it, though she didn't normally smoke. Her hand was so unsteady that he had to hold it still to light her cigarette.

They sat in silence for a few moments and then Helen glanced up to find Colin's eyes thoughtfully on her. She attempted a smile, but it was a poor effort, and he said gently, 'What's wrong, darling? It's something more than concern for people you've never seen, or for a man you've only met two or three times – an acquaintance, really.' He stubbed out his cigarette and knelt on the floor beside her. Touching her bare arm, he said, 'You're cold. Shall I put the fire on?' He reached out to push a plug into place and a small electric fire began to glow into life. 'Better?'

She nodded. 'Thank you.' Then she put her hand in Colin's and said, 'I'm all right now. Sorry I got so upset. It's because I'm not used to things like hurricanes. I'll take them more calmly when I've been here a while.'

'Perhaps that's it.' He was still looking at her so fixedly that she bent her head on the pretext of tapping ash from her cigarette. 'Helen,' he went on, 'what would you say if I told you I wanted to break our engagement?'

Her head jerked back and she stared at him. 'You want to–? Is that what you want, Colin?' His question had come as such a shock that it almost drove her worry about Paul Strang from her mind.

'Yes, Helen. That's what I want.' He spoke in a flat, expressionless voice, but his brown eyes were full of tenderness. 'It's the only thing to do, isn't it?'

'I – don't know.'

'I think you do, my dear. You know you don't love me – not as I want you to – not as I love you. So it's no use pretending, is it?'

'But I do love you, Colin. We could be happy together. We have our work–' He needs me, she was thinking. And I need him now.

He smiled a little sadly. 'Work? That's not enough. I'm glad you care for me, and I'm proud, too. But again, it's not enough.'

'People do get married with no more than we have–'

'I know, and it might have worked out pretty well. If one of the partners were not in love with someone else.'

'Colin! What do you mean?'

'Did you think I wouldn't guess?' he asked affectionately. 'I think too much about you not to know you're in love with Paul Strang.'

'Oh, Colin, I'm sorry!' All her fear and despair were released in a flood of tears, and she covered her face with her hands.

He took her in his arms and comforted her as if she were a child. 'Don't cry, dear. These things happen. I tried for a while to pretend it hadn't happened; to believe we could marry and be happy, but it's no use. Come on now, let me wipe your eyes. There! Everything will sort itself out, you'll see.'

She sniffed. 'I don't see – how it can.'

'Just you trust your Uncle Colin,' he said.

She managed a weak smile and then leaned against him, eyes closed, waiting. How long they remained like that, she did not know. Eventually, the door opened and they were both instantly alert.

The man Colin had called Ted came in looking lugubrious. Helen gripped Colin's hand tightly as the New Zealander said, 'No joy from Caroline yet. A call just came through from Prince Albert. The doc left there a week ago to visit Charlotte and Caroline Islands before coming on here.'

'Have they heard from him – on Prince Albert Island – since he left there?' Helen asked in a strained voice.

'No. But that's not unusual. He doesn't radio to base unless something unexpected crops up on the job, and they don't contact him unless they want him to alter course for any reason. They're trying to find out where he is now, and will get through to me as soon as there's any news. I'll get back to the switchboard now.'

Colin said: 'Thanks, Ted,' and then looked at Helen. 'Let me take you home, dear. It might be hours before we hear anything more.'

'I must wait. Please.'

She curled up in the armchair and finally dropped into an uneasy sleep, haunted by a strange kaleidoscope of dreams that made the expression on her pale young face change constantly. So powerfully vivid were they that when she half-opened her eyes and saw Paul Strang's dark face, she was certain she was still dreaming.

'Paul. You're safe. Darling,' she breathed, and drifted back into sleep.

She awoke again, fully this time, and he was still there. She blinked, and he didn't disappear. He was smiling, a tender, warm smile. Then he spoke, softly.

'Hello there. How are you feeling now?'

'I – I'm all right – thank you, Doctor.' She sat up straight, pushing back her hair. She must collect her wits, yet with him perching casually on the arm of her chair, looking at her with an expression that – well, that was anything but business-like or formal – it was extremely difficult to think calmly. And when he said, 'Doctor? It was "darling" a moment ago,' and put his hand under her chin to raise her face so that she had to look at him – then it became utterly impossible.

Her cheeks flamed. 'Oh, goodness! I thought I dreamed that!'

'I'm glad it wasn't a dream, Helen.'

'You–? But you – can't mean–?'

'I mean that I love you, dearest Helen, and I hope with all my heart that you love me.'

'I do, Paul. You know I do. So much.'

In his arms, with his lips on hers, all questions and doubts floated away on the surging tide of ecstasy that engulfed her. For this brief space of time she gave herself up completely to the sheer delight of love.

Suddenly, the thought of Colin broke the spell, and she turned away. Paul asked what was wrong.

'Colin,' she said. 'Has he gone?'

'Yes, darling. We had a talk, and then he went home. I told him I'd take care of you.'

'Everything's happened so quickly,' Helen said, frowning a little. 'I still feel as though I haven't properly woken up.'

He smiled and kissed her eyes lightly. 'I'll try to straighten things out for you,' he replied.

He explained how his boat had managed to avoid the main force of the hurricane and get to a sheltered bay on an uninhabited island, where it stayed until the worst of the storm was over. Arriving at Victoria, he had come at once to the radio station to send a message letting his colleagues on Prince Albert know he was safe, 'and of course, I found you and Fraser here,' he went on. 'You were asleep, so I talked to him and naturally congratulated him on his engagement, though it wasn't easy, feeling as I do.'

She looked up at him with wonder. Could this really be happening? Oh, it would be too cruel if Fate had let her taste the wine of enchantment only to dash the cup from her lips.

She murmured his name, and as if he guessed something of the turmoil in her mind, he drew her close and held her to him. 'When Colin told me the engagement was off – that was all he said – I didn't know what to think. He went home, and I stood watching you. You looked so young and sweet, curled up like that. Then your eyes opened and you said, "Paul. You're safe. Darling", and I knew that you loved me, too.'

'Did you know – before then – how you felt?' she asked shyly.

'I didn't know until you told me you were going to marry Fraser. Then I suddenly realized why I kept thinking about you, why I resented Fraser's being with you every day – oh, a lot of things I'd found excuses for, were all at once made clear.'

'I thought you – cared for Anna Wakefield.'

'Poor Anna! She's a child, a beautiful child who wants a lot of attention. She amuses me, that's all.'

'Does she love you?'

'Not me, or anyone else. She's too absorbed in herself.'

Helen hesitated a moment and then asked about Colin. 'Was he all right when he left?'

'He will be fine. You've done a great deal for that young man, you know. He's mature enough now to take disappointment without becoming bitter,' Paul said thoughtfully. 'And he's found a greater interest in his work through you. Yes, he'll be all right.'

'I must stay and help him until we get the right person to take my place.'

'Yes, darling. I knew you would want that. But we will be married soon, won't we?'

She kissed him. 'Very soon, please, darling.'

The publishers hope that this book has given you enjoyable reading. Large Print Books are especially designed to be as easy to see and hold as possible. If you wish a complete list of our books please ask at your local library or write directly to:

Dales Large Print Books
Magna House, Long Preston,
Skipton, North Yorkshire.
BD23 4ND

This Large Print Book, for people
who cannot read normal print,
is published under the auspices of

THE ULVERSCROFT FOUNDATION